BRAD GRINNED LOVINGLY AT HER.

"Mother warned me about women like you. She said you'd take advantage of me, use my body, then discard me like a worn shoe."

"Mother was a smart lady," Jeni quipped, patting his cheek. Lord, he was attractive. His appeal, just lying there, was enough to turn her heart inside out and rekindle the warm glow in her innermost core. She reached for his mouth again, covering it with her parted lips.

"Superman?" she murmured dreamily.

"Yes?"

"Can we go flying again. . . ?"

KASEY ADAMS is an incurable romantic who loves to travel, paint, and above all, write. She also enjoys numerous other activities, including working as an Emergency Medical Technician and teaching kindergarten. Ms. Adams is the mother of two grown children and lives in California with her husband. She is the author of three other Rapture Romances, *Purely Physical*, *Winter's Promise*, and *Untamed Desire*.

Dear Reader:

We at Rapture Romance hope you will continue to enjoy our four books each month as much as we enjoy bringing them to you. Our commitment remains strong to giving you only the best, by well-known favorite authors and exciting new writers.

We've used the comments and opinions we've heard from *you*, the reader, to make our selections, so please keep writing to us. Your letters have already helped us bring you better books—the kind you want—and we appreciate and depend on them. Of course, we are always happy to forward mail to our authors—writers need to hear from their fans!

Happy reading!

The Editors
Rapture Romance
New American Library
1633 Broadway
New York, NY 10019

AN UNLIKELY TRIO

by
Kasey
Adams

RAPTURE ROMANCE

NEW AMERICAN LIBRARY

NAL BOOKS ARE AVAILABLE AT QUANTITY DISCOUNTS
WHEN USED TO PROMOTE PRODUCTS OR SERVICES.
FOR INFORMATION PLEASE WRITE TO PREMIUM MARKETING DIVISION,
NEW AMERICAN LIBRARY, 1633 BROADWAY,
NEW YORK, NEW YORK 10019.

SIGNET, SIGNET CLASSIC, MENTOR, PLUME, MERIDIAN AND NAL BOOKS
are published by New American Library,
1633 Broadway, New York, New York 10019

First Printing, September, 1984

1 2 3 4 5 6 7 8 9

PRINTED IN THE UNITED STATES OF AMERICA

To Joe,
my anchor, my comfort, my love

Chapter One

❧

Jeni blinked furiously, trying to stop the stinging in her eyes, but the cloud of smoke was too thick. For the third time in ten minutes, she gathered up her writing materials and moved her folding chair to a different spot within her campsite. She rubbed her eyes to clear them, glancing furtively at the source of her problem.

Actually, she thought with well-hidden amusement, the problem is the man, *not* the fire. Her long auburn hair was pretty well protected by a plaid scarf, but she knew she was going to smell disgustingly like a toasted marshmallow if he didn't get his fire started properly— and soon.

Looking like a handsome lumberjack obviously wasn't enough to equip him for camping, she mused, as the man poked at the smoldering wood in his fire ring. He added more damp logs and what little flame he'd managed to coax to life was promptly quenched.

Standing with his hands squarely on his trim hips, his sleeves rolled up to expose strong forearms, the man shook his dark head and stared at the smoky mess that refused to burn.

Jeni smiled, covering her smirk with her hand. It wasn't polite to laugh, but the scene was growing funnier by the minute. The disgusted look on the man's face was a cross between defeat and determination, with just a touch of wry humor. He seemed to acknowledge, at least partially, the absurdity of his situation.

Red and gray coals glowed beneath the iron grate in Jeni's fire ring. James would be proud of me, she thought, feeling only a slight pang of loneliness. Their marriage had been a good one, cut short by his death in the line of duty, and Jeni had come to grips with her grief in the natural course of going on with life. It still hurt, and he would always be with her, but the pain had become a gentle treasuring of memories that now brought more joy than sorrow. All she knew of the outdoors had been learned from her husband during their short but happy time together, and Jeni felt his presence most when she, too, was close to nature.

Settling herself comfortably into her chair, she resumed writing the letter she'd begun before the drifting smoke had disturbed her. After a moment, she closed her eyes and sighed, visualizing the frail-looking, dark-haired child she'd come to love. "Oh, Timmy," she whispered, seeing in her mind his pleading, dark eyes, "I wish you could have come with me." Pausing, she added that thought to her letter to the little boy, signing it, "Your new Mom, Jeni." Folding the paper, she slipped it into an envelope to mail later. Linda would read it to him.

A twinge of regret shot through Jeni. Maybe she'd been wrong to leave Tim. Maybe she should have skipped her whole vacation and stayed home to wait for the papers that gave her temporary custody as a foster parent until the adoption came through. Taking a deep breath, she straightened. No. Linda had been right about the whole thing. As Jeni's sister, she could feel close to the problem, yet still view it with a more objective eye than Jeni herself.

"And I *do* need to be here," Jeni whispered to the towering firs dotting the alpine forest. "I've missed this beautiful place."

Another dense cloud of smoke drifted by her and Jeni coughed, turning toward the annoyance from the neighboring campsite. He was *never* going to get the fire started with all that heavy wood piled on top of the barely warm kindling. She was moving before her mind was truly made up. Approaching the large rocks delineating the place where the two campsites met, she stood quietly watching, fanning the smoke away from her face with both hands. A soft cough escaped from her irritated throat.

The man looked up, saw her, and smiled sheepishly. "Hi."

"Hi," Jeni said, ducking a fresh cloud of wafting smoke. "Having trouble?"

"Nothing that a well-trained troup of boy scouts couldn't fix," he said lightly. "There seem to be some serious gaps in my earlier education."

"Like fire-starting?" His smile warmed her, his twinkling dark eyes reminding her of Timmy's.

"How'd you guess?"

Jeni stepped over the rock barricade. "Something in the air told me," she said with a laugh.

"Ah, I see," he said, feigning a seriousness he obviously didn't feel. "I notice your fire seems well in hand."

"My husband's a boy scout," Jeni answered, absently twisting the gold band on her left ring finger. Speaking of James in the present tense was a habit she'd quickly developed for her own protection after his death. It gave her a feeling of safety and kept unwanted suitors at arm's length. "The lady might be a widow," she'd often explained, "but the lady is definitely *not* available."

The man extended his hand in greeting. "My name's Brad. Brad Carey."

Jeni put her much smaller hand in his and gripped it

firmly, surprised at the forthright way he returned the handshake, the way he continued to gently press her fingers when there was no further need. "Jeni O'Brien."

"And your husband?" Brad asked, scanning the campsite over her shoulder. His questioning look seemed to be asking why he'd seen no sign of the man.

"James," Jeni replied. She withdrew her hand from Brad's, but not before a remembered warmth had begun to nag at the edge of her consciousness. Still, there was something different about Brad's touch. No calluses. That was it, she realized. His hand was too smooth. She stared at the hand that had so recently grasped hers. The flesh was firm and muscular, and there were fine, curly, dark hairs on his arm, hand, and the backs of his fingers. Definitely a masculine hand, but so out of the ordinary. Not at all what she'd come to expect from a man who looked like Brad did. My God, she thought, his nails were even clean and well trimmed.

"Is something wrong?" Brad asked, rubbing his hands together, then holding them up for his own inspection.

"Uh, no." His question pulled Jeni back to the present.

He was looking quizzically down at her. A pretty lady, he thought. Slightly built, but no softie judging from her firm handshake. Her auburn curls tumbled out from under her scarf in a soft cascade over the shoulders of her red down vest. A *very* pretty lady, Brad had just decided, when her green eyes met the deep brown of his. Brad looked quickly away. He wasn't in the habit of coveting other men's wives, and he felt uncomfortably transparent when she stared into his eyes.

Jeni, too, suddenly felt ill at ease. Perhaps she shouldn't have intruded on the man's privacy.

He turned back to his fire and busily made matters worse. "I don't suppose you'd know what's wrong here, would you?" he asked innocently.

She stiffened. Why was it that men repeatedly equated women with helplessness? "I built my fire," Jeni said, gesturing toward her camp.

"Oh. I see." Standing, he faced her. "Would you show me, then? I'm familiar with the principles of combustion. It just seems . . ." He shrugged.

"Sure." Jeni took a long stick and pried the grate off the firepit. "First, you can't do it all at once. You have to get the kindling burning well, then add smaller pieces of wood until the bed of coals is hot enough to light the heavier, damper logs. It can be done. See?" She dragged most of his earlier effort out of the way and began to re-lay the fire.

Brad crouched next to her. "If you say so. You're the teacher." His hands were clasped between his knees while he gave her his undivided attention.

"Actually," Jeni volunteered, striking a match, "I'm a probation officer. Or I was until recently," she added with a twinge of bitterness.

"Probation officer? A little thing like you?"

The fire flared, and so did Jeni's temper. She drew herself up to her full five-and-a-half feet, smoothed her jeans, and glared down at him. "I am neither little, *nor* helpless, Mr. Carey." Her leg was growing uncomfortably warm from its proximity to the flames. "Observe your fire."

"Touché," Brad replied. "Look," he said slowly as he rose to stand, "I'm sorry if I offended you. It was a natural reaction and I said it before I thought."

She relaxed slightly, tossing wood on his fire. "It's okay. Happens all the time. I should be used to it, but it still bothers me." Jeni paused. "I'm very good at whatever I do."

Watching his fire flare to life, Brad didn't doubt her, and he said so.

"Thank you. Usually people remain skeptical till they've known me longer."

"Ah, but I'll bet they've never seen your expert boy scout act. The fire's fantastic!"

Jeni laughed. "True. But I seldom build fires in my office to convince the rest of the world I'm proficient at it."

It was his turn to chuckle. "Good. I'm sure your co-workers are grateful for that." Brad eyed his blazing fire. "Tell me when it's ready to roast hot dogs, will you?"

Her eyebrows arched in disbelief. With all that fancy equipment, he was going to cook hot dogs?

Flipping up the lid on an enormous ice chest, Brad extracted a plastic package. "The legendary tubesteak," he said. "I didn't want to get in over my head trying to cook till I'd mastered a few basics. This is my first experience at camping." His excitement was almost childlike.

"Do tell." Jeni couldn't help smiling.

Brad took it good-naturedly. "Shows, huh?"

She nodded, fighting to keep from laughing.

"My brothers-in-law helped me buy the equipment. To tell the truth, I'm still not sure whether I need all this stuff, but they were the experts, so I trusted their judgment."

Jeni looked around his well-stocked camp. "I'd say you could live comfortably for months." The gear stacked neatly on the table and ground would have taken her years to accumulate, and undoubtedly the blue and white camper hooked to the back of a new pickup truck contained even more modern conveniences. And the man was planning to eat hot dogs!

Brad was watching her mental inventory. "Too much?" He seemed to value her opinion after the fire incident.

"No. It's more than we've managed to collect in a lot of

years of camping, but it's all relative. If you use it, it's not overdone."

"Good. I'd hate to have spent the money foolishly."

Jeni cocked her head to one side and glanced nonchalantly at him. "Did a rich uncle die and leave you a fortune?" she asked flippantly.

"No. My grandfather." His response was serious, with a hint of sadness in his voice.

Oh, damn, Jeni thought. Why did I have to say that? "I—I'm sorry."

Brad straightened, thrusting his hands in the back pockets of his jeans. "It's okay. It was a long time ago." In answer to her questioning look, he simply said, "And a long story." But over, finally, he told himself, at last.

"Listen," Jeni went on before considering her gesture carefully enough, "I have some fresh-caught rainbow trout. Let me give you a couple. It sure beats hot dogs."

Smiling, Brad nodded. "True. However, I'm afraid I'd ruin them. Then my neighbors," he gestured at her campsite, "would have wasted good trout."

"Oh." Her first impulse was to invite him to eat with her. He certainly seemed to be interesting company and having planned to bring Timmy along, she had plenty of food for two. But Brad thought James was with her. Darn. This was the first time her pretense had gotten in the way of something she really wanted to do. The big lug was likely to sit at his table eating burned hot dogs while she dined on sumptuous trout and felt guilty she hadn't taken a chance and invited him.

Jeni decided quickly. There could be any number of reasons why James was temporarily absent from camp. She'd simply make excuses and enjoy her dinner. It was a rescue of sorts, she rationalized. Anyone as inept as Brad needed all the help he could get, and she could teach him to cook over a campfire while she prepared dinner.

"Why don't I fix them for you?" she asked politely. "There's plenty."

Hesitating, Brad scanned her camp. Perhaps her husband was asleep in their tent. It was quite possible he wouldn't welcome company for dinner. If I had a woman like that, Brad thought, I wouldn't want to share her for a minute. "Are you sure?" he asked. "I mean, won't your husband mind?"

The warmth of sweet remembrances flowed over Jeni. "No," she said with a tenderness borne on those memories. "I'm sure James would want you to come."

Jeni banked the fire, adjusted the grate, and called to Brad. "Cooking lesson starts momentarily."

Haltingly, he stepped over the rock barricade. "You're sure your husband won't mind?" he asked, looking left and right. "I feel like an intruder."

"Don't," Jeni said brightly. "Have you ever scaled a fish?"

"If that's anything like scaling Mount Everest, no."

"It's not, and I doubt you've done either. Am I right?"

Brad nodded, a small smile curling the corners of his strong, sensitive mouth. "You're getting to know me pretty well, Mrs. O'Brien."

Handing him a board, a knife, and the ice-cold trout, Jeni began to explain the procedure.

Brad reached for the first fish and found it slipping unceremoniously out of his hands to land with a plop in the dirt at his feet. "Damn. That little devil's slipperier than a class of seventh graders bent on smoking in the restrooms." He picked up the fish. "Now what?"

"You wash it off and try again," Jeni answered, averting her gaze to keep from smiling at his struggles.

He laid the thoroughly rinsed fish on the table, then bolted over the rocks and began rummaging in a knapsack in his own camp. "Got it."

"What's that?" Jeni asked.

Brad proudly placed the new board and shiny tool on the table. "A proper fish-scaling outfit," he said. "I wondered what this clip was for till my little friend here slithered out of my hands." Stringing the trout onto his scaler, he quickly finished the task she'd given him. "There. Amazing what modern technology can do for a job as old as time, isn't it?"

"I suppose you washed them after you finished," Jeni said flatly. There was nothing wrong with the tools she'd given him, and she didn't intend to fawn over the scaler *or* the man.

"Clean as a whistle," he said happily. "Now what?"

Jeni smiled to herself. She could understand his feeling of accomplishment. James had tutored her in much the same way and she'd felt a surge of pride every time she'd learned a new skill. It was fun being on the other end of the experience.

"Let me see." Careful inspection revealed an excellent job. "Good boy," she teased, "you'll make the troop yet." Some boy, she mused; he's probably past thirty.

Brad casually saluted her, his hand going on to brush back a shock of dark hair. His brow furrowed and he brought his hand to his nose. "Ugh. You forgot to tell me I'd smell bad!"

This time, Jeni laughed heartily. "You'll live."

"Undoubtedly." Brad joined in her laughter. "Especially once I've tasted of the fruits of my labors."

The sizzling trout rested together in a large iron skillet, and Jeni began to set the table.

"I'm the proud owner of a plastic tablecloth. Would you like to cover the table first?" Brad had come to stand behind her and Jeni was startled at his nearness, and the coursing warmth she felt begin to flow through her.

"Uh, no, thanks." She ran her hand over the rough planks. "If we cover this and then set something down where we can't see the uneven surface, it can tip over. I've done it." Out of small talk, she fell silent.

"Okay." He was watching her closely as she prepared the table. Only two plates were in evidence. "Am I no longer invited?"

She caught her breath. Of course. He was expecting James, and she hadn't yet worked out her excuses for his absence. "Uh, no. My husband won't be with us for this meal."

Brad didn't seem to notice her uneasy demeanor. "I see. And you're sure he won't mind your feeding me?"

"Of course not." She laughed nervously. "I often bring home stray puppies or kittens."

"Or campers?"

"Or campers. If they look lost enough."

Leaning back, Brad grasped one knee, lacing his fingers together. The sleeves of his plaid wool shirt were still rolled up, exposing his strong forearms. Dark hair curled from the V in his collar front, echoing the deep coffee color of his hair and eyes.

"I'd hoped that by dressing the part, I'd be able to pass for an outdoorsman," he said.

"It takes a little more than that," she replied quietly. "External appearances can be very deceiving."

Air whistled through his lips. "You can say that again. Are you really a probation officer?"

Jeni shrugged. "I was until recently. I've just changed jobs."

She seemed perturbed, almost angry, Brad noted. He tried to overlook her altered mood, and asked, "Your husband didn't worry about you?"

"We met through our jobs—his on the police force and mine in the rehabilitation department."

Brad stared off across the campground. "I see."

"I take it you're a teacher," Jeni deduced.

He blinked. "What? Good God, I hope it doesn't still show!"

Laughing, Jeni assured him he looked anything but studious. "It was your comment about seventh graders sneaking a smoke in the restrooms," she went on. "You're either a teacher or a cop, and I think I'd recognize the latter."

He held out his hands in a gesture of acceptance. "Guilty, or at least I was. I'm an ex-teacher, as of a few weeks ago."

She found that harder to understand than his obvious lack of experience in the wilds. "Why? When you're in a position to help so many kids, why stop?"

"Now you sound like my family and colleagues."

"Sorry."

"It's all right. I've explained it so many times I could do it in my sleep." He rose and walked over to the fire. "Today's kids don't care, for the most part. They're drones, Jeni, and the occasional one who does want to learn can't make up for the feeling I get of pounding my head against a brick wall the rest of the time." He paced restlessly back to the table and nibbled on a corn chip. "It was getting so I hated the thought of going to work."

Brad paused, considering whether to go on, then decided to confide in her. After all, she was just a passing acquaintance, and it would feel good to get the rest of it off his chest. "I hated the kids, too," he confessed with a hidden sorrow. It hadn't always been that way, he recalled, but strange things happened to a strong-willed man who was forced into a lifestyle of someone else's choosing.

"You're not serious!"

He shrugged. "The way I feel now, I'd just as soon never have to deal with another kid again."

Jeni looked so repulsed, he was afraid she was going to throw him out, then and there. Brad hadn't asked her if she had children, he'd just assumed that, because he didn't see any, she had none. Looking at her, Brad could easily picture her as a mother. "I haven't told that to anyone else," he said quietly, "because I expected the same reaction I just got from you."

If that's the way he feels, Jeni thought, thank goodness he's quit. How awful for his students to have a teacher who felt that way. It was bound to affect his classes.

"Do you and your husband have——"

Jeni cut him off with a crisp, "No." She hadn't forgotten Timmy, but neither had she forgotten the waste she'd felt when James had died before they'd found the right time to begin a family. She took several deep breaths. Feeling guilty for having denied Timmy, she set about to rectify her quick, negative remark. "But I'm adopting a boy."

"In these times, lady, that takes guts," Brad said rather sarcastically.

"I've never been short on those, either, Mr. Carey," she replied flatly. "I'm tough. Ask the juveniles in my old caseload, if you doubt me." She carried the trout to the table, her back rigid, her jaw set. No one could say Jeni had fallen apart under any of the stressful circumstances in which she'd found herself. Proud of her strength, she wore it like a mantle, isolating herself from the storms buffeting her. Only one man had ever penetrated her protective barrier, and that man was James O'Brien.

It had taken a great deal of courage to pursue the adoption of Timmy, especially once she'd realized it was going to cost her her job, the career she'd worked so hard to make for herself. Still, if she could save one small boy from the fate of his brother, Alex, then it was worth all her sacrifices. Poor Alex, she thought. Just one more juvenile offender who got the message too late. There was a rough road ahead for him, but thank God she'd gotten to Timmy in time. How could Brad not care, not keep trying? Some teacher!

The delicious aroma of the fresh trout was making Brad hungry, and the first bite was ambrosia. "After tasting this, Jeni O'Brien," he said gallantly, "I wouldn't doubt anything you told me. It's marvelous!"

She relaxed slightly. "Thank you." After all, what difference did it make if Brad liked children or not? Lots of people didn't, and since he was out of teaching, he could do no more harm. A born crusader, she was glad he'd made that decision. She told him so. "If you hadn't decided to stop teaching, I'd be trying to talk you into quitting right now."

Brad swallowed and asked, "Why?"

"It's not fair to the kids, that's why. A teacher who really hates his job can't do it well."

"I did all right."

"Ah, but all right isn't good enough. Don't you see? A job done with less than total commitment is only half done."

He nodded. "I do see. That's why I got out as soon as I could."

"Why did you go into it at all?" Surely, he must have suspected he'd dislike the occupation.

"It's a long story," he said wearily, evasively. There was no need to rehash the complicated details, even if it would raise Jeni's opinion of him. What was done was done. He'd paid the price for everyone and kept his family from splitting into opposing factions as he'd feared might happen if he had contested the unfair stipulations in his grandfather's will. Best of all, there was still time to start over. At thirty-three, he could finally begin to live the life he'd come to want with a single-minded longing.

Jeni was speaking. "So, what will you do now?"

Smiling sheepishly, Brad regarded her across the nearly finished meal. "You won't laugh?"

His smile was contagious. "No promises. But I will try to control myself."

Brad grinned. "Fair enough. I want to buy a pizza parlor and learn to run it."

Jeni's imagination was running rampant and she did giggle.

"You promised."

"Sorry, it's just . . ." Even her fingers pressed to her lips couldn't stem the tide of laughter.

"Okay, Jeni, let's have it. What's so funny?"

"I—I was imagining a place like that with no young people," she explained. "You know, senior citizens as bus boys. Then you could put a sign on your door that said, 'No Children Allowed.' "

"Very funny." He'd begun to chuckle. "Maybe I need to soften my outlook."

"Or choose another business. What was your second choice."

Brad could hardly contain himself. "An amusement park, but I can't afford the kind I want."

The next thing that popped into her mind was even sillier. "How about a roller rink?"

"Super! Think of the money I'd save on skates. With no kids, I'd only have to stock adult sizes."

"Right." Jeni tossed a bag of marshmallows at him. "Grab a stick and let's have dessert."

Moments later, he'd returned from his camp with two long, shiny skewers. "How about these?"

She shook her head incredulously. "Well, I don't think it'll taste as good without the wood flavoring, but I'll try it." Threading a soft, white marshmallow on the metal spear, she handed it to him. "Go for it. I don't suppose you've ever straightened a coathanger to roast marshmallows either, have you?"

"Have I missed something else important?" Brad

asked pleasantly, his gaze following her graceful movements.

"Probably," she replied. "Uh, do you realize yours is on fire?"

"What?" Brad was absent-mindedly watching her while his marshmallow became a charred remnant.

Laughing almost uncontrollably, Jeni pointed to the flaming end of his stick. "B—blow!" she managed to say as he withdrew it from the embers. It was too little, too late.

Brad wasn't as hysterical as Jeni, but he was laughing too. "I take it there's something else you haven't told me."

"Good grief. I didn't think there was a grown man in the world who hadn't roasted marshmallows," she stammered quickly.

"In your world, maybe not." He was shaking his hand as the hot, melted sweet clung to his fingers. "Ouch!"

Withdrawing her lightly browned marshmallow from the fire, she laid it on a paper plate and went to him. He'd washed his fingers, and two angry red welts were beginning to show where the hot stickiness had refused to let go. Jeni reached into her ice chest and grabbed a handful of the cracked ice. "Here. Put this on the burned places now and they'll be okay. It looks like second-degree."

Wincing, he did as she suggested. "I suppose you know what you're doing medically, too," he said.

She bowed slightly. "I'm an EMT—Emergency Medical Technician—in California. Want to see my card?"

"Never mind. I'd believe anything you said at this point." He picked up his skewer. "Can I do this one-handed?"

"You are determined, aren't you?" Jeni observed. To his credit, he was game, she mused.

"Damn right. No little white puff ball is going to get the best of me."

"Okay." She brought him her marshmallow. "It's supposed to look like this. Lightly browned on the outside and melted inside. If you're careful taking it off the stick, you can keep the skin intact and save your fingers."

"Now she tells me."

Jeni made a silly face at him, then extended the warm, crispy marshmallow toward his mouth. "Open up." Had she known how the simple act would affect her senses, she would never, *never* have done it.

Brad's lips parted to accept the gift, and as he did his eyes met and held her gaze.

For Jeni, everything seemed to be happening in slow motion. Her fingers dropped the marshmallow into his mouth and withdrew, but not before they'd softly grazed his lower lip. She saw it tremble slightly in unison with the shiver that shook her. As his mouth closed, Brad's tongue involuntarily licked the traces of sugar off his lips and Jeni found herself rooted where she stood, unable and unwilling to move away from him.

His own reaction surprised Brad. Good God, he thought, the woman's married! And what a fool her husband must be to neglect her the way he has. For all her self-sufficiency, there was a childlike vulnerability about her that screamed for protection. Brad's gaze swept her face, settling on her wide-eyed expression. She was scared, and it was written all over her. No, Jeni hadn't tried to seduce him. Their sizzling attraction to each other had been totally accidental, and now she didn't know what to do about it. Well, he did.

Brad stepped back, still clutching the melting ice in his burned hand. "Tell your husband," he said firmly, hiding the unsteadiness he felt, "that I appreciate your hospitality. I think I'll check my fire and turn in. Good night."

Jeni stood, still holding the marshmallow stick in one hand as she watched him step over the barrier. He was well out of earshot when she finally whispered, "Good night."

Chapter Two

ও৲

It wasn't a particularly good night. Jeni dreamed a dream
of pure longing. It was the kind of experience she'd often
had after James's death, when the hurt was fresher and
the loneliness deeper. A long time had passed since the
last dream, and she'd thought herself free of the uncon-
scious need.

Exhausted from her restless sleep, she dressed at
dawn and wandered out into the alpine meadow. In her
very biased opinion, Cedar Breaks was one of the most
beautiful places in Utah, and she reveled in the fresh,
piney smells borne on the morning air. The surface of the
reddish ground was beginning to dry to a thin crust
around the clumps of tiny wildflowers scattered over the
hills. Her boots crunched across the rolling ridges. If the
flowers didn't get some rain soon they'd die for lack of
water, she thought, remembering from experience that
summer storms were common in the high country. The
flowers would recover.

But would *she*? she wondered. Had she been fooling
herself into believing she'd relegated her memories of
marriage to her past and was able to go on living nor-
mally? Something in the dream had disturbed her
deeply—was it the strong arms cradling her, the gentle
kisses, her own responses . . . ? Jeni hugged herself and
shuddered. It had been like all her earlier dreams, but

somehow different. No amount of pondering helped her pinpoint the problem. As elusive as a whisper on the wind, the details necessary for understanding it escaped her. She'd almost grasp the secret and it would slip out of her mind before she could identify it. What was so special about the dream? Why couldn't she recall?

Thoroughly frustrated at her inability to remember fully, she trod back to her camp.

"Morning."

Coming through the trees, her mind on her dream, she'd misjudged the distance and was standing in Brad's camp. Jeni quickly recovered her composure, shaken at being in the wrong place. "Morning. I guess I'm slightly off course."

Brad smiled graciously. "Good. It's nice to see you're not totally perfect."

She smiled. "Far from it, I'm afraid."

Glancing toward her camp, Brad asked, "Is your husband up yet?"

"Uh, no. I mean—I'm afraid you've missed him again. Why?"

He pointed to a stack of gear on the end of his picnic table. "I was hoping he'd give me some help with that, and maybe a hint as to where you've been catching those fish we had last night. I'd like to try my hand at fishing today."

"Panguitch," she said succinctly.

"Geshundheit," Brad joked.

"I didn't sneeze." Jeni smiled. "Panguitch is the lake where we've always fished. The name is Indian for 'big fish.' It's about fifteen miles down the mountain."

"Would you mind showing me?"

Jeni's heart leaped, beginning a wild, runaway pounding until she saw him pull a folded map out of his gear. Of course, he hadn't meant for her to actually *take* him, she

lectured herself sternly. Besides, she didn't want to. She
didn't.

He spread the map on the table. "Where?"

Leaning over the map, she carefully traced the route.
Brad was so close behind her, looking over her shoulder,
that she almost turned and fled, not from fear of him, but
from her own unsettling reactions to his nearness. Her
finger stabbed at a point on the west shore of the lake.
"When you get there, you can rent a boat." She stepped
aside, crossing to the other side of the table. She had to
put something between them. "The best fishing is here,
or here."

"Why?" It seemed a sensible question to Brad.

"The fish are there," Jeni explained as if she were talking to a child younger than Timmy.

Brad was genuinely surprised. "You mean, they're not
all over the place?"

Jeni shook her head. At least her pulse had returned to
what felt close to normal. "What did you teach, anyway?"

"English," Brad said. "Would you like me to dangle a
participle for you? I'm really quite good at it."

"I'm sure." She looked at his fishing pole. "Have you
fouled the line or did a spider build a web in your reel?"

"No spider. I did it all by myself."

Lifting the pole, Jeni said, "Congratulations. It's a
splendid job."

"Thanks."

"You're welcome," she said. "Here. Hold the end of
the line and I'll see what I can do."

Dutifully, he complied as she backed across the
campsite playing out the line and working at the snarl.
When the line was fixed, she returned the pole to Brad.

"Keep your thumb here when you cast," she told him
patiently, demonstrating. "Got that?"

"I hope so," he said. "Wish me luck."

Watching Brad climb into his truck and start to drive

away, Jeni was suddenly seized by memories of her dream. What was pushing at her subconscious to get out? She shook her head slowly and turned, entering her own camp. After a good, basic breakfast she'd go fishing again. Last night's dinner guest had polished off her extra catch and this area was the best trout fishing for hundreds of miles. No use wasting the opportunity, now that her limit of fish had been eliminated.

"And what about your neighbor?" she asked herself aloud. "You don't want him to think you're following him." Jeni laughed at herself. Panguitch was an enormous lake. Even the best spots left plenty of room for everybody. She probably wouldn't even see Brad Carey. Quickly, she squelched the tiny voice inside her that said, "Too bad."

Jeni's little red Honda bounced lightly over the gravel drive leading to the lodge. She noticed Brad's truck with an unexplainable jolt of excitement. Lecturing herself about the folly of caring at all, she parked, rented a boat from Mrs. Andrews, the matronly lodge owner, and started for the dock, her receipt in hand.

Cool and blue, Panguitch Lake was nestled among the rolling hills, in picture-postcard perfection and tranquility.

The young blond man on the floating dock greeted her warmly, as usual, glancing at her name on the rental ticket. "Hi, Mrs. O'Brien. You eat all those trout already?"

Jeni smiled down at him as he checked the motor on the boat she'd rented. "Well, I did have some help. How's the catch running today?" She peered at the faded embroidery over his shirt pocket, "Ronnie."

The boy shrugged. "Too soon to tell. I haven't seen many people trolling yet, so I guess the fish are biting."

"Super." Trolling was a pain, Jeni thought, especially

for one person. Managing the tiller and keeping the lure moving at just the right speed could prove very taxing. She only resorted to it when there was no other productive way to fish.

Shading her eyes, she gazed across the lake at the spot she'd recommended to Brad. The boats looked so tiny. "Have you had many customers, today?" she asked, stepping into the boat while Ronnie held it close to the weathered dock.

"Not many."

Jeni considered asking about Brad, then changed her mind. It was silly to worry. He'd be fine. He was a grown man, and she wasn't his keeper, after all. She smiled to herself. If anyone needed a nursemaid in the situation in which he'd placed himself, Brad Carey did. Oh well, she sighed inwardly, I'm here to fish and to get away from everything, not babysit a wayward ex-English teacher.

Stepping carefully over the slick aluminum seats that bisected the yellow boat, Jeni put the motor in neutral, choked it, and pulled the cord. It started on the first pull.

Ronnie released the chain on the bow. "You headed across to the cut, Mrs. O'Brien?" he asked, referring to a bared portion of the eastern shore. Local fishermen coveted the spot as the best on the lake.

Jeni nodded, calling to him over the roar of the motor. "Yes. Why?"

The boy pointed that direction. "I've got a customer stuck halfway there and I can't leave to help him till my brothers get back. Would you mind seeing if you can do something?"

Waving in agreement, Jeni put the motor in reverse, easing between the other boats and out into the lake. It gave her a feeling of pride that a boy like Ronnie trusted her expertise with the boat enough to ask her to help out. He was of the new generation of men, she observed, the ones who'd been raised to accept someone on qualifications and skills alone, and not reject a capable person just because she was a *she*.

Shifting into forward, Jeni twisted the throttle control in her left hand, gunning the motor and raising the boat's bow as she sped toward the stranded fisherman. Swells ruffled the lake surface ahead of her as her craft noisily slapped the water. Peering ahead she saw a lone fisherman bending over the rear of his boat, surrounded by unnaturally calm, greenish waters.

"Damn!" Jeni veered away just in time to avoid a similar fate, circling the boat's hapless occupant. No wonder he was stuck, she thought. The fool had steered right into a bed of underwater plants, and now it looked as if he was about to tumble headfirst into the water.

"Hey," she called loudly, "need some help?"

The man straightened with some difficulty, tipped his hat off his forehead, and stared at her slowly passing craft. "I'm not sure," he called sheepishly. "This is getting a little repetitive."

"Morning, Mr. Carey," Jeni mocked in a friendly taunt as she cut her engine, "did you get stuck in a dangling participle?"

Brad laughed, leaned slightly off balance, and caught himself with one hand on the edge of the boat. "It's a dangling something, Mrs. O'Brien. Any suggestions?" He raised a knife in his right hand. "I've been hacking away for what seems like hours."

"Did you lift the propeller shaft?" she asked, knowing he hadn't, but trying her best to be polite.

"The propeller shaft?" Brad's dark eyes darted from Jeni to the motor and back several times. "I should have known there'd be a better way." He sank wearily onto the hard aluminum seat. "Okay. How?"

Jeni patiently explained about the release lever that would let him bring the motor forward into the boat, thereby lifting the shaft and propeller free of the water.

Quickly locating the lever, Brad did as she'd instructed. Slippery green tendrils had wound tightly around the whole underwater mechanism. Cutting weeds off, he dropped the last of the offending greenery overboard. "I hate to sound redundant," Brad called to Jeni, "but, thanks."

He tucked the knife into its sheath. If he lowered the prop back into the water, he knew he'd be right back where he started, too fouled to move. So now what? The oars? Of course, Brad concluded, reaching beneath the rims of the seats to release the yellow oars. Paint flaked away from them, sticking to his hands. They obviously hadn't seen recent use.

Jeni waited to see what he'd do. He definitely wasn't stupid, she decided, watching him work through his current problems. Nor, was he inept; not really. He was like a child in his lack of practical knowledge. Some child, her subconscious nearly shouted. That, my girl, is a full-grown, very attractive specimen of manhood.

Jeni swallowed hard, forcing her gaze away from Brad's broad-shouldered frame. She blushed as her eyes darted back to his bared forearms, trim waist and hips, strong hands . . . Looking at him was a pleasurable experience, she acknowledged reluctantly. Very pleasurable.

He sensed her focused concentration, turning to face her. "How far do I have to row to be out of this mess?"

"Oh, uh—past the quiet water." Jeni pointed. "See how the lake is rougher where I am? The plants keep the swells down."

Brad glanced at the spot where he'd been trapped. It was only about fifty feet in diameter. "Outside there?" he called, just to be doubly sure.

"Yes." Jeni started her motor. "Follow me." She pulled away slowly to keep her wake from giving him more problems than he already had.

Rowing silently, Brad quickly learned how to get the

most forward motion from the oars without turning the boat. His rhythm was becoming smooth and powerful by the time he was free of the weeds.

Jeni was waiting. She cut her engine, allowing her boat to drift close to his.

He lifted the oars from the water. "The Lone Ranger, I presume," he said, smiling modestly.

"Something like that," she replied.

"Where do I go to apply for Tonto's job?" Brad asked.

"Uh, well, I . . ." Jeni wasn't sure what he was asking, nor was she sure what her reaction would be if he were to ask to stay with her.

That was exactly what he wanted. "I just wondered if maybe—I realize it's an imposition, but—well, I'd hoped that perhaps you wouldn't mind if I sort of tagged along."

His smile was open and honest. Whatever attraction Jeni was feeling for him didn't seem to be reciprocated. And why should it be? she chided herself. As far as he's concerned you're a married woman. Besides, what's wrong with two people having fun together? Why should it matter if one happened to be male and one female? Lots of friendships were based on shared interests without sharing a bed. She blushed behind her sunglasses. Why in the world had she thought of Brad and bed together? That was preposterous! And why shouldn't she let him come along?

"Okay, Tonto, but I get to lead," she quipped, starting her engine.

After several tries, Brad finally got his motor to fire and fell into line behind her. She was one special lady, he mused, watching her silky auburn hair blowing in the wind; a self-sufficient individual with a rare consideration for others that he found refreshing. It must have a name, this quality of Jeni's. Kindness, was the closest he could come.

And what of her mysterious husband? Brad wondered.

What was it she'd said his name was? James, he nodded to himself. They were adopting a child. The man must exist if that were . . . Wait a minute. Jeni had said *she* was adopting a child, he realized. *She*, not *they*.

He watched her navigate the eastern shoreline. She could have lied. Why did he have trouble believing that? he asked himself. Perhaps because he liked her, truly *liked* her, and couldn't imagine negative qualities in her character, he decided seriously.

Jeni cut her engine, gesturing to Brad to do the same. The two aluminum hulls clunked gently together and he held her boat next to his while she dropped her anchors, then did the same for him.

"Okay, Tonto," she said lightly. "We're here."

Grinning eagerly, Brad opened his tackle box. "This, you won't have to show me," he said. "I read up on trout fishing before I left. I'm an expert—at least on paper."

She cast a sideways glance at him. "Uh, I hate to break this to you, but those lures are for fly fishing in streams, not bottom fishing in lakes."

It was obvious he didn't believe her. "You're kidding."

"Sorry. No." Jeni held out her hand. On the palm was a small, white, powdery object. "Have a marshmallow."

"I'm not hungry." Brad was morosely surveying his expensive collection of useless trout flies. Jeni's laugh distracted him.

"This is for the fish, Tonto, not you."

"Marshmallows?" Brad took the soft sweet. "I suppose the fish will take them untoasted."

Jeni flushed, remembering the roasted marshmallow, Brad's lips, and her strange reaction to him. "They aren't fussy," she said quickly. "Start with that and if it doesn't work, we'll switch to cheese bait."

He closely watched her rig her pole. "Could I borrow one of those swivels, a weight, and a plain hook?"

Chuckling, she handed him the things he'd asked for. "Who was your keeper before I came along?"

Brad took her comments good-naturedly. "No one. I sort of muddled through." Pausing, he made a fair cast, playing out line until he felt his sinker hit bottom, and sat down straddling the bench seat in his boat. "Do you remember reading, when you were a kid, how the Indians sent a young man into the wilderness to prove himself? Well, that's kind of what I'm trying to do by being here."

"You're no kid," she observed in a friendly tone. "What took you so long?" He'd pulled the brim of his hat over his eyes and Jeni could no longer see his expression.

"I had prior commitments," he told her, sighing. "I'm thirty-three and I feel like a case of arrested development. While other boys were out playing baseball, building tree houses, or learning to fish, I was already well ensconced in a stuffy classroom being groomed for the role I was to play in life."

"As a teacher?"

"As a member of academia, yes. My father, and his father before him, saw me as the successful educator I finally became." His voice held a sad inflection.

So that was it, Jeni mused. And why not? Most people thought they chose their own careers when in reality they were usually influenced by outside sources. The only difference in Brad's case was that he saw it clearly. Still, he seemed to her to be a strong-willed, confident man. Why had he put up with being manipulated if he'd known it was happening? It didn't make sense.

"Why wait so long?" she asked, casting her line away from his.

"You mean to quit? I told you. I had commitments. A lot of others were depending on me." Before he could tell her more, there was a quick jerk on his line. The tip of his fishing pole bent over, sprang back, then bent in an inverted U shape. "Jeni! Help!" he sputtered.

She'd been aware of the strike before he was. "Keep tension on the line or you'll lose him," she said authoritatively. "That's it. Reel in the slack."

Rocking with the rhythm of his pull against the struggling fish, Brad watched his line being dragged in circles and swirls, cutting a crazy, zigzag path through the deep lake.

Jeni was winding up her line to get it out of his way.

The iridescent body of the rainbow trout broke the surface of the water in a graceful arc, then dove once again.

"Wow! Did you see that!" Brad shouted.

"You'd better stop admiring that fish and get your net ready or you'll never land him." She tossed a green mesh net to him. "Here. Use mine."

Jeni would have bet even money Brad would fall into the water before he got the fish out. With one arm holding his pole over his head, he struck the foaming water with the net, scooping again and again before he netted and landed his trout.

"Got him!"

The man was exuberant, she noted happily. It gave her great pleasure to see the wide grin lighting his face. Naturally, she would have felt that way about anyone she'd guided, she convinced herself hurriedly. Brad was nothing special to her. Nothing at all.

The breadth of Jeni's smile nearly matched his. "Good for you, Tonto," she praised. "Now, what are you going to do?"

"Huh?"

Shaking her head, Jeni passed him her creel. "Drop this into the water, *after* you've tied it to the boat, then slip your fish through the door at the top."

He followed her instructions to the letter, watching

the freed fish swim lazily around inside the metal basket. Finally, he turned his gaze to her.

"It doesn't bother you to fish?" he asked.

"No. I figure the fish has a chance to turn down my bait and swim away—if he's smart enough."

"Ah. A battle of wits, eh?" Brad was baiting his hook. "And who usually wins?"

She cast over the far side of her boat. "I'd say it's a toss-up. Some days I've been skunked; others, I've caught my limit of eight and had to stop."

"So, that's why you wanted me to eat your fish," Brad teased. "You had your limit and wanted to fish some more."

Jeni agreed. "You've found me out, Tonto," she said. "There goes my good-guy image." She popped a clean marshmallow into her mouth.

"Hey, you're eating the bait," Brad scolded.

"I saved some for me," she corrected. "You just fish and let me do my thing or I'll cut you loose and you'll have to make it on your own."

"You'd do that to me—after all we've been through?" His face sagged wistfully in a feigned pout.

Jeni found herself taking his clowning too seriously, but she wanted to stay with him, to trade silly, teasing comments and wile away the warm, summer day. There was an easy pleasure in Brad's company, a relaxed friendship she hadn't experienced since . . . Suddenly, her dream came roaring back into her consciousness and she knew what it was she hadn't been able to pinpoint before. For the first time in years, the ethereal man in her arms hadn't been James.

The rest of the morning, Jeni managed to engage the bulk of her concentration on the blue sky, the cool lake, the brushy hills surrounding the shore, the flaking yellow paint on the boats' hulls—anything but Brad. She ate the last marshmallow on their way back to the dock.

The two largest trout in the creel were his, and he jogged to his truck, returning with a camera. "Would you mind?" he asked her politely. "If I never do this again, I'd like a photo to remember it by."

"Sure." She put down her tackle box and other gear. "Go stand over there with your fish."

Sighting him through the camera, she was surprised to feel her heart do a little syncopated flip-flop. Jeni gritted her teeth at the inference her body was making. This was dumb, and totally out of the question. She didn't want a man, especially Brad Carey. Charm couldn't substitute for all the other qualities she required in a man—her man. The love of children, for one thing. Besides, after James, she'd made up her mind to go it alone. That was working, so why mess up a good deal? she asked herself. And why were these thoughts crowding into her mind? Why now? Most of all, why Brad?

She was overtired and lonely, Jeni told herself. She missed Timmy, and camping again in Cedar Breaks had brought back old memories. It would have happened with *any* man she'd run into up here. This one's not special.

Brad's wide, carefree smile filled her view. He looked so—so dear, standing there proudly displaying his catch. A lump in her throat appeared without warning. Why in heaven's name did she feel like crying? she wondered, growing angry with herself. She was twenty-eight, not a silly child with a crush. Had she been out of circulation for so long that she didn't know how to act naturally around a single man? Treating Brad the way she had been was definitely a mistake, she reasoned plausibly. He'd fit too easily into the only gap in her life, letting her imagination take over and giving far too much importance to their tenuous relationship.

Jeni snapped the shutter, advanced the film, and took two more pictures to be sure he'd gotten his memento.

Alone in her little car, driving back to camp, the thought-provoking quiet seemed to press in on her. Yes, she admitted, Brad *was* an attractive man. Attractive to her. Warmth coursed through her as she visualized his gentle strength, his dark, handsome looks, his eagerness and acceptance of her instruction.

Why had she insisted for so long that her games of pretending James was alive were innocent? She'd hidden behind him, hadn't she? Jeni absently chewed her lower lip. That was exactly what she'd done. It had kept her from having to deal with any new relationships. It had been a protection of sorts, too, but there was more to it than that. Now, she saw she'd used the ruse unfairly. Fear of danger was one thing; fear of everyday living quite another.

She was waiting for Brad when he parked his truck. "What do you say we cook them together, since we caught them that way? Seems a shame to break them up now, doesn't it?"

Eyebrows raised, he slammed the truck door. "I don't know, Jeni," he said skeptically. He was beginning to look forward to seeing her, being with her, and that was dangerous.

"Don't you want to? I mean, I thought we'd gotten along pretty well up to now."

Brad grew serious. Taking her left hand, he raised it between them, his fingers playing with her wedding band. "See this, Jeni?" he said.

Her guileless green eyes looked up into his.

"You're married. I think we'd better call a halt to our friendship."

"Why?"

"Because I like being with you," he said. "I like it too much for my own good. And I won't take another man's

wife, even if he doesn't appreciate her like he should."
Brad glanced over her shoulder at her deserted camp. "I
see he's not here today, either."

"He would be if he could, Brad. For years we were
inseparable." Tears gathered in her eyes, not because of
her long-ago loss, but because she'd seen a glimmer of
caring from another person. The strong facade she'd
always presented had kept anyone else from expressing
real support. The lady with the iron constitution didn't
need others, did she?

Brad watched her, his heart going out to her for all the
wrong reasons. "And now he's left you, hasn't he?" he
demanded crossly. It was a damn good thing he hadn't
met O'Brien, he thought. The man deserved a good
punch in the nose.

Tilting her chin up with two fingers, Brad apologized.
"I'm sorry, Jeni. I know it's none of my business. I just
can't understand how a man could treat you like that.
You're his wife, for God's sake."

Jeni saw the harshness in his eyes turn to a gentleness
as he gazed down at her. How would he feel about her
once he knew? she agonized. Still, she had to tell him. It
was time to stop playing games, to stop pretending.
"No," she said in a low, raspy whisper, "I'm not James
O'Brien's wife, Brad. I'm his widow."

Chapter Three

Brad remembered very little about dinner. They'd eaten, like the previous night, but his thoughts boiled through his mind, pushing aside any recollection of the mundane.

A widow. Jeni was a widow. Why had she led him to believe otherwise? he wondered, staring at the paneled ceiling of his camper. And how many of the other things she'd told him were half-truths? He laced his fingers behind his head. Suppose he'd known she was free and single from the beginning? Would he have joined her for dinner? The answer came loud and clear from his subconscious. No. He had enough current problems to resolve without complicating matters with a woman.

Well, it had been fun being with her, knowing her, but that was all over. Whatever chemistry there had been between them would cool if he kept his distance. It was a simple solution and it should have allowed him to relax and sleep. However, for some unknown reason, his decision gave him no peace. No peace at all.

Jeni sighed, pulling the top of her sleeping bag closer around her neck. What a strange reaction, she recalled, thinking about the moment when Brad had fully realized what she'd said. His fingers had jumped from her face as if he'd been scalded. It was ironic, she reflected. All along she'd been afraid men would try to take advantage of her if they knew she was single. Instead, the first man she tells, the first one she cares even a little about, drops her like a hot rock.

Perhaps she shouldn't blame him too much, Jeni thought. After all, she had sort of lied to him to start with. Maybe his trust was too shaken to recover. Besides, what difference did it make? He was only a passing acquaintance, a stranger.

Unfortunately, the fact that he was a gentle, handsome, endearing stranger hadn't escaped her notice, either. How marvelous it would be if . . .

"Jeni, my love," she quickly lectured herself, "your hormones are kicking up. You'd best pull yourself together and concentrate on making a home for Timmy." Agreeing, at least in principle, she snuggled farther down into the bag, closing the top flap to preserve her body warmth. Consequently, she didn't feel the strong winds or see the gathering thunderheads blot out the moon and stars.

The first huge drops of rain pattered loudly against the metal shell of Brad's camper. Still wide awake, he lifted the edge of the heavy window curtain. Through the darkening night, he could barely see the outline of Jeni's small orange nylon tent. She'd assured him she'd pitched the tent on high ground, expecting rain. A bright flash of lightning gave him a clearer picture. So far, she seemed to be secure enough. He'd unconsciously begun to count following the flash, barely reaching two before the crash of thunder. That was close, he thought. Too close for comfort.

Swinging his legs off the bed, Brad pulled on his jeans and drew back the curtain over the camper door. Another lightning flash showed Jeni's tent, wet but standing firm. The wind had reached a frightening velocity. Gusts swayed the camper while heavy rain beat against the windows and door. How could she possibly stay dry in a tent? he worried, as one more flash lit up her campsite.

When Jeni realized a storm had come upon her, she carefully pulled away from the sides of the tent to leave the surface tension undisturbed. She'd be fine, she knew, as long as everything held together. Storms in The Breaks were common and sometimes severe, but always short. All she had to do was hold her breath till . . . A gust stronger than the others hit her tiny tent, pulling two corner stakes out of the now sodden ground.

"Damn," she muttered. Holding the loose corners down from the inside proved impossible. She struggled into her jeans, her short nightgown flowing over the top, and crawled out into the storm. Her slicker was in the car, along with her hammer to replace the stakes. And her car keys? They were in the rapidly collapsing tent.

Brad flung open the door to his camper. "Jeni! Get in here!"

Her hair was plastered to her head and neck, her clothes soaked to the skin, while she struggled futilely to pull the tent back into shape.

"Jeni! Don't be a fool. Get in here." The commanding note in his voice demanded her attention.

"No! I can fix it," she called loudly in his direction. A new lightning strike came only seconds before the thunder and she thought she heard the sound of splintering wood close by. That convinced her.

Brad's door was still open when she made a dash for the camper and he closed it behind her. "About time. You're drowned, lady."

"S-s-sorry," she stammered, shivering uncontrollably. "I've n-never seen a storm this bad up here."

Brad handed her a towel. "Stand there till you dry off some more and I'll give you a change of clothes."

Clothes. Jeni glanced down at her soaking gown. Her breasts were clearly visible through the wet fabric and

Brad seemed to be taking it all in. She couldn't stay there with him, she thought in a panic. Not all night! Suddenly, the lightning frightened her far less than the man.

Twisting around in the cramped confines of the narrow hall, she grabbed the knob and threw open the door.

"Jeni!" Brad's cry was a mixture of surprise and anger. "Jeni!"

Stopping in the clearing, she could see only dimly. The thick curtain of driving rain confused her and she whirled in circles trying to get her bearings.

"Jeni!" Brad's strong grip on her arms brought her to a halt. "Where do you think you're going?"

"I-I don't know." She tried to break free. "Let me go." Thunder nearly drowned out her frantic plea.

"Jeni," Brad shouted, "don't be a fool. Why did you run?"

"I—I'll stay in my car," she insisted, trembling.

Crazy woman, he told himself, trying to brush the rain off his face so he could see her. "Okay, okay. Give me your keys and I'll unlock it for you." He held out his hand.

"They're . . ." She pointed to the jumbled, soggy tent.

"So, come back to the camper."

"No!"

"Are you afraid of me?" Brad demanded. "Well, are you?"

Her head moved in a barely perceptible nod, eyes downcast. Rivulets of water coursed through her hair and flowed down her body, robbing her flesh of heat as Brad's nearness had robbed her of self-assurance.

Brad shook her by the upper arms. "Look at me, Jeni. Do you expect me to take advantage of you in there? All I'm trying to do is get us both out of the rain. There's nothing else to it. Understand?" He was shouting again. His voice lowered as he said, "I won't harm you. I promise."

Something in his manner calmed her. Perhaps it was his words, perhaps the loosening of his grip. Nodding, Jeni followed him back to his camper.

In the soft glow from the overhead light, she let herself look covertly at her rescuer. Brad was trembling as badly as she. With no shirt on, he'd taken the brunt of the icy rain on his bare skin and his flesh glistened as he moved to get her another towel. Water dripped from the dark curls pasted to his forehead, but he seemed more concerned with her welfare than his own, she noticed.

"Here. Dry your hair," he told her gruffly. "I'll get you some clothes." He held an old gray sweatshirt over his shoulder, keeping his back to her. "Put this on."

"In here? Now?" Jeni asked. "But——"

"But nothing," Brad cut in sharply. "You're wet and freezing, and so am I. I promise not to peek, but hurry up, will you?"

Jeni stripped off her wet clothing, pulling on the oversized sweatshirt quickly. It hit her halfway between her hips and knees. "Okay," she said, dutifully turning her back to Brad and winding the damp towel around her wet hair.

He found dry jeans and shorts, wriggling into them as quickly as he could, and slung a towel around his neck.

"Okay." Brad turned to find her watching him. Nothing had prepared him for his reaction when he saw her. Unadorned, she was even more beautiful than he'd thought before. The brightness of her wide emerald eyes seemed to fill his consciousness. Her look was one of almost childlike trust, open and unafraid. Dwarfed by the shirt he'd given her, she looked like a street urchin he'd somehow rescued and then bathed.

A shy half-smile curled her lips. Still chilled, Jeni shook with a barely perceptible shiver. "The Lone Ranger, I presume," she said.

Brad blinked as water dripped from his hair. "And you must be Tonto."

Her grin broadened. "You got it, Kemo Sabe."

Good God, he thought, doesn't she know how she looks, what she's doing to me? Look at her. As innocent as a babe. When he'd told her there was nothing special about her coming into his camper he'd meant it, hadn't he? Yes, his conscience screamed, yes! But now, looking at her standing before him . . .

Jeni stepped a little closer. Taking the end of the towel he had draped around his neck, she gently blotted the water from his face. It *was* good to be there with Brad; to know she'd be safe and dry no matter what happened outside; to be sheltered; to relax and for once to not have to be quite so strong, so self-reliant.

She freed the towel. "Sit down." As Brad sank silently onto the edge of a narrow padded bench, she began to vigorously towel-dry his hair.

Her closeness, the sweet odor of her warmth, was driving him crazy.

"That's enough," he said sternly, getting to his feet. "I'll get out some blankets for myself and give you my sleeping bag." Rummaging through a lower cabinet, he withdrew several clean blankets. "The bag is on the bed."

Jeni knew his sleeping bag would be far warmer than the blankets and she felt guilty accepting it. "Really, I . . ."

Brad reached for the bag to straighten it. A strange look crossed his face.

"What is it?" she asked when he didn't speak.

"Wet," was all he said.

Her gaze darted to the door. Of course. They'd left the door open when she'd run into the rain like a silly fool. It was her fault. "I—I'm sorry, Brad."

He clutched the folded blankets to his bare chest, seemingly lost in thought.

"I can still use it, can't I?" Jeni ran her hands inside the soft lining of the sleeping bag. It was soaked through. "Well, I guess there's just one thing to do," she said lightly, stripping the damp fabric from the bed and reaching for the blankets. "Are these all you have?"

Brad nodded, watching her, wanting her, and wondering if he was going to be able to keep his ridiculous promise not to touch her.

She arranged the blankets on the bare mattress, then climbed up onto the bed and rolled herself in the top blanket. "See? It'll be like bundling was in the colonial days. The blankets will keep us decent and we'll still have each other's warmth. Come on." She patted the bed next to her. "I won't bite."

He shrugged, turned off the light, and joined her, feeling her soft, warm hands helping him adjust his blanket. Curling up on the narrow bed, Brad kept his back to Jeni. Wouldn't his brothers-in-law have a good laugh if they knew about this, he mused cynically. Here he was, in bed with a beautiful, desirable woman, and he had his clothes on and blankets carefully tucked between them.

Listening, he heard her breathing slow and deepen. Poor thing. She'd been through a lot in the last hour. The fires of his desire for her began to cool and he could appreciate the sensibility of their situation. Two mature adults seeking shelter didn't have to develop a sexual involvement to share a bed, did they? Of course not. The only thing between them was a blanket, not a relationship. She was simply another human being in need of his help.

He'd almost convinced himself it didn't matter whether or not Jeni was a man or a woman when, fast asleep, she rolled halfway over, fitting the curves of her body to his and snuggling closer.

Brad drew in his breath sharply as her arm slipped around him. Damn it, he cursed. He did care. More than his sexual attraction to her, he admitted to himself, he also cared about her as a person.

Jeni's hand found the warm, bare flesh of his chest, caressing him tenderly. Intertwining his fingers with hers, Brad stopped the sensual movement. She was asleep, he knew, and not responsible for what she was doing to him. He fought to slow his rapid breathing.

Murmuring, Jeni drew him closer, her senses responding with remembered passion to the presence of a strong, masculine body in her bed.

He could turn and take her, Brad knew, and she'd probably be his before she truly awoke. But he couldn't do it, he couldn't betray her trust. Why not? he asked himself over and over as her warmth penetrated the blankets. Why not? She's just another woman, isn't she?

Brad clutched her hand tighter. No. Jeni O'Brien would never be just another woman, he concluded. She was special.

Jeni was only vaguely aware she was touching Brad. A healing mist shrouded her mind, cushioning her first few steps away from her past, her fond memories of her marriage. Resting her cheek against his shoulder, she rubbed it back and forth lightly, reveling in the smooth, warm texture of his skin, the unmistakably masculine odor and feel of him. Her lips found his bare flesh, kissing him heedlessly. A sense of déjà vu tugged at her conscious mind. This was her dream—a recreation of her deepest desires. Her eyelids fluttered, then opened. She was hugging Brad! With his back to her, she couldn't tell if he was awake or asleep. Certainly, if he'd been awake he would have stopped her, or . . .

Jeni pulled slowly away from him, tucked her arm back inside her blanket, and rolled over. Brad hadn't moved, hadn't said anything. She sighed, deeply relieved. Thank goodness he'd been asleep. She pressed her fingertips to her lips, remembering. He'd felt so good, so right, and her body ached to be near him again, to touch him and be held close. Jeni shivered violently, shaking the whole bed.

"Are you still cold?" Brad whispered groggily.

No words would come to her.

Another shiver seemed to answer his question and he turned, drawing her into his embrace. "Go to sleep, Jeni," he said. "I'll take care of you."

Her first reaction was to remind him she could take care of herself. She was independent, self-sufficient, and—and it felt so good to be held close, to be cossetted, even if the advent of morning would bring an end to her belonging there.

Relaxing in Brad's strong arms, she let herself mold to him as he hugged her back to his chest, much the same as she'd found herself holding him.

Oh Lord, she realized with sweet agony, it had been so long. How could she not have seen how terribly lonely she'd been? Jeni drew a ragged breath, fighting swelling tears, and felt Brad's embrace tighten, comfortingly, reassuringly around her.

He was gone when she awoke. Stretching slowly, Jeni opened her eyes. At the sight of the inside of Brad's camper, she remembered where she was, and why.

A nervous flutter went through her like the wind through the quaking aspen leaves, stirring her awareness of Brad's night-long presence. Pulling the blankets up around her neck, she noticed both were now tucked securely around her. Brad had done that, she realized with a pang of gratitude. He hadn't simply left her, he'd carefully covered her with his own blanket before he'd gone outside.

Jeni hugged the gray wool blanket to her, drinking in

the lingering odor of the man who'd spent the better part of the long, trying night with her. He really was gallant, she decided. After all, she'd seen him struggle with the news of her widowhood, then open his camper to her in spite of his obviously negative feelings about the whole thing. That took a special kind of person.

A brisk knock on the door startled her.

"Hey, Tonto. You'd better get up soon," Brad called through the closed door.

Up, meant dressed, and dressed meant dry clothes. "I—I don't have anything to wear."

"Just like a woman," he teased. "Never has a thing to wear." He paused. "I'll get you something out of your car."

"The big blue suitcase in the back seat," Jeni shouted. "Please."

Brad was back quickly, opening the door a small crack. "You decent?"

"As decent as I get this early in the morning," she told him wryly. "My mouth feels like the inside of an ancient sneaker."

"How lovely," he replied, grinning at her. "You do look kind of wiped out."

"Thanks. I needed that." He set the suitcase on the small table opposite the bed. "Speaking of wiped out, how's my camp?" she asked, knowing he'd have had to venture into it to get her car keys and clothing.

Brad drew his hand over his chin, a day's growth of stubble giving his face a roguish, shadowed look. He shook his head. "Get dressed first. Then we'll go through it and see what has to be done."

"That bad, huh?"

He forced a smile. "I'm the wrong one to ask. I'm the city-bred novice, remember?"

"True," she agreed. "But you're bright enough to recognize a disaster when you see one."

Brad shrugged. "You're right. It's a mess." Turning, he left her to dress.

Jeni wriggled into an old pair of jeans and pulled on a soft, pale pink and blue sweater. She folded the sweatshirt Brad had given her and laid it gently on the rumpled bed, stroking the worn fabric lovingly. Twisting the wide gold band on her finger, she held out her left hand, staring at it. Perhaps it *was* time; everything had a proper season, a preordained order that defied change.

She slid the gold band off her left hand, hesitated only a fraction of a second, and slipped it on her right. It wasn't being unfaithful to James's memory to transfer the ring, she reasoned. Nothing could ever deprive her of the memories of the first man who had shown her what love could be. It was simply time; time to go on, to take stock and look ahead, not dwell in the past, however lovely it had been. A telltale mark remained on her left ring finger, a reminder of the band that had occupied the space for too long.

Jeni peered at the small oval mirror on the wall at the foot of the bed. Egad! Her hair looked like the wreck of the Hesperus! And shoes. She had nothing to put on her feet. Swinging open the door, she called to Brad, "Hey, Tonto."

Chuckling, he answered her. "Oh, no, you don't. I was the Lone Ranger last night, so *you* have to be Tonto today."

"Okay, okay. Did you see my sneakers in the car? My boots were in the tent and I don't want to go 'clop-squish' all day."

He was rummaging through her things. "Any hints?"

"Nope. The last time I saw them was when I packed. They're blue."

Brad finally produced one of the shoes. "How about hopping on one leg?" he gibed, still digging. "Ah, got it."

With both shoes in hand, he held them up for her to see. "What're they worth to you, Tonto?"

"Let me put it this way," she replied, "either you give me my shoes or I won't rescue you from yourself anymore."

Faking chagrin, Brad tossed her the sneakers, one at a time, watching while she quickly put them on.

Before Jeni was halfway to her camp, she'd assessed the situation. One word described it—ugh. "What a mess," she said disgustedly. "Everything I had out is soaked."

Helping her repitch her tent, Brad was amazed at how well she was taking the minor disaster. He would have expected tears, or at least a good, loud tirade, but Jeni just went to work. He found that quite amazing.

Her sleeping bag was so soaked it was difficult for her to lift it without his help. They piled the wet clothes and belongings on the end of the picnic table.

"How about using my truck to haul all this stuff down the mountain and dry it in a laundromat?"

"Modern conveniences?" she asked wryly. "We could hang it over a tree branch."

"And what *year* were you planning on using it again, Jeni? Look at the water in your bed. Do you really think it'll dry up here, as cool as the weather is, in one day?"

"No." She eyed her little car. "I guess I can unload some of my other gear and pile the wet things on the floor."

"And suppose it rains again while you're gone?" Brad asked. "Look, I have some stuff to dry, too." He made a face at her. "It seems someone left my door open during the storm."

Jeni feigned a childish pout. "Says who?"

"I have my sources—spies everywhere," Brad told her. "Let's take my truck. The floor is already wet from that raggedy puppy I took in last night."

"Puppy? Raggedy! Hah," Jeni exploded.

Brad was laughing easily. "Take a peek at yourself in a mirror and tell me you're not a little ragged around the edges," he teased.

"You're no Prince Charming yourself, Kemo Sabe," she observed. "Did you break your razor?" Rummaging through a damp knapsack she found her hairbrush, tackling the rain- and sleep-caused snarls in her hair with a vengeance, grimacing as the stiff bristles caught and tugged.

Brad grabbed the brush from her. "You'll be bald in no time if you keep that up. Turn around."

A strong hand on her shoulder and a desire to see what he was up to kept her in place while he gently worked through the tangles in her thick hair. Tingles of electricity seemed to shoot down her spine as his ministrations spoke to her of a gentleness, a kind of tender loving.

Laying aside the brush he smoothed her hair with both hands. It was fine, like silk, a deep burnished gold that reminded him of an autumn sunset. His touch lingered.

And you were going to keep your distance, he remonstrated, not let yourself get involved. His fingers traced the length of her hair, then came to rest on her shoulders, feeling them relax and soften under the weight of his hands. "I—I think we'd better go if we're going to get it done and be back before the day's gone," he said to break the fascination he sensed.

Jeni rose slowly, barely nodding, and helped him load the truck. There was no reason for her to feel sad, yet she found she did. Brad was beginning to mean something to her. She couldn't let that happen, not with her prior commitment to Timmy. Someday, she might choose a man for herself and a father for the boy, but that man would have to be as ready to be a loving parent as she felt she was. A man who admittedly hated children wouldn't

do. She glanced at Brad, clenching her jaw determin-
edly. No, it just wouldn't do.

The laundromat in Cedar City offered enough separate
machines so that they could wash and dry most of their
things at the same time.

Several small boys and one tow-headed little girl raced
barefoot up and down the aisles, their round faces
decorated with an odd assortment of various sticky
substances.

Jeni watched Brad's expression. There was no doubt
he was less than delighted about the children's presence.
The girl fell and Jeni helped her up.

"You *do* like those little rug rats, don't you?" he asked
cynically.

"Don't you?" She'd hoped he'd relent and show her a
more open attitude.

"Sorry. I'm up to here with kids." He held his hand at
chin level. "I told you."

"Well, I know, but don't you think they're cute?"

Brad gestured disgustedly toward the boisterous children. "They need a good lesson in acceptable behavior
for a public place," he said. "If they're going to act like
animals, they belong outside."

"Animals don't treat their young with the disdain *you*
show, Mr. Carey," she shot back.

"*Animals* don't permit their offspring to get out of line
in the first place. One misstep and they give the young a
good hard cuff or nip them. Animals are more civilized
than a lot of people."

"I'm glad you weren't in charge of raising me," Jeni
said defiantly.

"Lady, if I had been, maybe you wouldn't be so confused about what it takes to bring up a child properly. I
shudder to think what's going to happen to you if your
adoption goes through."

Jeni was livid. "What do you mean, 'if'? It's going through!"

"You have no idea how tough it's going to be, do you?"

"Tough?" She jumped to her feet, hands on her hips. "I'll tell you about tough, Brad Carey. Tough is giving up my career to pull a kid like Timmy off the streets. Tough is battling unbending bureaucracy till you're blue in the face and almost broke. Tough is watching Timmy's brother, Alex, being sentenced again and knowing Tim'll be next if you don't do something." Tears of anger and frustration pooled in Jeni's eyes, misting her view of the man who was regarding her seriously, silently. "And tough is making something happen that everyone you know—I mean *everyone*—has said is impossible. You *bet* the price is high. I've paid it so far, and I'm not about to quit."

Brad rose slowly and left her to check on the dryers. His face was to the wall, watching the sleeping bags tumble over and over in a noisy blur of color, when he said quietly, "And tough is a little lady who cares more than anyone I've ever met. Tough is named Jeni O'Brien."

Returning to her, Brad reached for her hand, glad she didn't pull away. "I'm sorry," he said quietly. "I had no idea this adoption meant so much to you."

Anger had used so much of her energy, Jeni was through fighting. She shrugged. "Well, now you know."

"Whew! I guess." Brad saw her begin to glower at him and he changed the subject. "The Lone Ranger and Tonto never argued, you know," he said brightly. "Come on. You check the smaller dryers and I'll see if the big one is finished yet."

He watched her cross the room. Such a strong will in such a delicate person, he thought with admiration. So, the adoption had cost her her job, had it? That must have been one hell of a decision to make, especially for her, since she'd been so involved in her career. This kid

Timmy must really be something special to make her fight for him like she had.

Brad thought back to some of the youngsters he'd befriended during his years of teaching. They were worth it, too, he mused. Perhaps the time he'd spent in the profession wasn't exactly wasted, just a part of a transition period in his life. Smiling to himself, he recalled the eagerness a few students had shown, the joy of accomplishment he'd felt when they'd warmed to his subject, glad to be learning. He'd begun to think of them as personal friends, rather than pupils.

Jeni noticed his detached air and pleased smile. "Hey, what's so funny? You look like the Cheshire Cat."

Brad's grin broadened. "Do I?"

"Uh-huh. What were you thinking about?"

"Old friends," he told her wistfully, "just old friends."

For some reason beyond her comprehension, Jeni wanted to go to him, touch him, run her fingers lovingly over the fine smile lines on his face. She swallowed hard. Old friends he'd said. Probably women friends, she concluded. A man like Brad had undoubtedly had his share of those. Her own misery at the thought surprised her. Why should she care? Jeni cleared her throat, fighting the answer. *Why*, didn't matter. The fact was, she *did* care, very much.

She busied herself stuffing dry clothes into a clean pillowcase. Damn—damn, damn, damn, she cursed silently. The man had major faults. Caring for him was insanity, pure and simple. A sensible woman wouldn't fall for him just because he was physically attractive, would she? Of course not. But, maybe . . . Jeni had never thought of herself as the type of person who could engage in a casual fling. It wasn't her nature. It went against all her inner convictions.

Besides, she reasoned, trying to put the idea of a romantic involvement with Brad out of her mind, he's not interested in me. The man spent the night with me, for God's sake, and never made one wrong move. Depressed, she thought over the scene in the camper. He'd been asleep when she'd inadvertently touched him. The memory of the warmth of his body centered as an ache in her abdomen. What might have happened if he'd been awake, aware she was caressing him? What if miraculously she got another chance?

Jeni plopped the pillowcase on the folding table where Brad was trying to sort his things from hers. "We can do that back in camp," she said. "How about lunch?"

"Sounds good," he agreed. Hoisting the heavy pile of clothes and sleeping bags, he headed for the door.

Jeni darted ahead to open it for him, holding it while he squeezed his burden through.

"Thanks."

"You're welcome," she said, her mind still actively remembering their time in the camper. Glancing at the bright blue sky, she asked in what she felt was a sexy voice, "Think it'll rain?" One peek at his face behind the pile of clothing told her he'd totally missed her insinuation.

Brad stowed the dry things in the camper. Her inane small talk was getting to him. The only time she'd *really* opened up and told him what she felt was in the heat of anger. He simply couldn't forget the depth of her emotion about the pending adoption. That boy must mean the world to her—and where did that leave him? he mused dryly. Nowhere, that's where. The lady was totally committed to Timmy. How did a man fight a rival like that? Brad turned the key and gunned the motor. He didn't. He was immersed in a no-win, Catch-22 situation.

Jeni noticed his silence, ceasing her attempts to make conversation and leaning her head back against the seat.

Terrific, she thought cynically, just peachy. I decide to make a pass and the guy starts treating me like a leper.

She sighed deeply. There wasn't a cloud in the sky. Not one blasted cloud. Even nature seemed against her. Jeni closed her eyes. Perhaps it was cloudy up in The Breaks. After all, it did rain often at the higher elevations, and if there should be another storm maybe Brad would invite her in again, and . . . And what? she snapped inwardly. What do you plan on doing, throwing yourself at him? Could she? More importantly, would she? she wondered anxiously. And if he laughed at her? Her breath caught in her throat. Darting a nervous look at Brad, she saw he was watching her.

"You okay?"

"Fine," Jeni lied convincingly. "How about burgers for lunch?"

"Suits me. Where?"

She pointed to a brightly painted hamburger stand. "There, looks good." As Brad parked the truck, Jeni scanned the sky once more. No clouds. No impending rain. And as she saw it, no opportunity for another chance with Brad. She was so caught up in her own morose mental ramblings, she didn't sense that he, too, was struggling, no less seriously than she.

Chapter Four

Except for a minor disagreement over the ownership of a pair of gray wool socks, Brad and Jeni easily sorted their clothing.

"They can't be yours," she insisted, holding one up. "Look at the size."

"Granted," he said, "but they *were* mine once. I think the dryer was too hot."

Jeni relented, studying the overly tight knit. "You're right. Here."

He folded the two socks together and pitched them her way. "You keep them. I'd never get them on, now."

Catching the tossed bundle, she joked thinly, nervously, "Gee, I don't know if I can accept such a personal gift, Mr. Carey. I mean, we hardly know each other."

"We've slept together, Mrs. O'Brien," he reminded her in a strangely grumpy tone.

She cast a sidelong glance at him, wondering if perhaps he'd been teasing her and she'd missed the pun. Brad's jaw was set, his manner tense and uncomfortable. He was deadly serious. But why snap at her? she wondered. He was the one who'd invited her in and insisted she spend the night.

"I think that's the lot, Jeni," he said, his dismissal unmistakable as he opened the camper door for her.

"Uh, thanks," she muttered, leaving the warm confines of his home-on-wheels. Even if he was sorry he'd befriended her, there was no reason for him to be so inhospitable.

Jeni stowed her dry clothes in her car, finished cleaning up her campsite, and unrolled her sleeping bag inside the still damp nylon tent. The bag would keep her warm, she assured herself, and she'd sleep in a sweatshirt for added heat.

It was nearly dinner time. Hunger should have been gnawing at her, but she found herself uninterested in cooking or eating. Brad hadn't left his camper, she noticed, discouraged and slightly upset with herself for her earlier romantic fantasies about him. So what if he didn't care or want her around anymore? Just because circumstances had thrown them together didn't mean they had to stay together. She needed to see him in the light of what he really was, her neighbor in a small, lovely Utah campground; nothing more, nothing less.

Jarred from her distracted mental wanderings by the arrival of a light green Forest Service vehicle, Jeni paid the three dollar nightly fee, making pleasant small talk.

An attractive young woman, the ranger wore her forest green uniform with the grace of a designer outfit, her Smokey the Bear hat perched squarely over long, silky blond hair.

"We have a program on local wildflowers in the visitors' center tonight," she told Jeni, handing her a receipt for her park fees. "It's at eight, if you'd like to come."

"Thanks. I'll think about it," Jeni said politely. If she went to the presentation, she thought, she might miss seeing Brad that evening. And did it matter? Oh yes, it mattered all right, she agonized, watching as the ranger stepped over the rocks and knocked on Brad's door. It mattered.

Jeni could tell from the blond woman's reactions that Brad was thoroughly charming her. Unreasonable anger gnawed at Jeni, making her more angry with herself than with Brad or the pretty ranger. She turned away when their mutual laughter reached her ears. The man wasn't going to get to her. He *wasn't*.

"Oh, no?" she muttered to herself. "Tell me another fairy tale, Jeni O'Brien. And make me believe it. I dare you."

Her campfire was blazing brightly by the time she saw Brad step out of his camper. It was nearly eight, she thought with inerrant accuracy, having checked her watch often during the long, dull evening. Jeni could feel her pulse begin to speed. Was he coming to see her? He must be, he . . . Brad turned away, starting up the dimly lit trail to the visitors' center. He was going to that darned show! she fumed. One look at a pretty ranger and he trotted off like a hound tracking a fox. What a, a . . . Words failed her.

Slowly, she came to her senses, poking thoughtfully at her fire. "And where does it say he's yours?" she asked herself. "When did you stake your claim to Brad Carey?" Her sense of fairness triumphed. He's not yours, Jeni, she acknowledged wearily, and the way it looks, he never will be. She'd come to totally accept that line of reasoning by the time Brad returned, a half-hour later.

Entering his camper, Brad switched on the electric lights. He'd hoped the show in the park headquarters would distract him, but it hadn't even come close to taking his mind off Jeni. Keeping his distance hadn't helped, either. If anything, it had made matters worse.

Brad shook his head, sank to the edge of the bed, and ran his fingers through his hair. He could change campgrounds, he thought, unwilling to make the final decision. He wanted her—yet he didn't. What did he want? he asked himself. "Damned if I know, anymore," he mumbled.

Disgusted with his own indecision as to whether he should put as much distance between them as he could, or go back to her and see what developed naturally, Brad unrolled his sleeping bag on the bed. Unzipping the side of the bag, he stripped off his shirt. There was no sense trying to think tonight. He'd get a good night's rest, then tackle the problem in the morning. A tiny speck of something white inside the sleeping bag caught his eye and he lifted the blue nylon flap aside, exposing the plaid lining. What the . . . ?

Brad's hand slowly reached for the lacy panties clinging to the lining, static electricity sparking as his fingers gathered the smooth material together. He held the feminine undergarment with almost a reverence. Pangs of arousal ate away at his control. As his fist closed tighter, he heard a low groan, hardly realizing it had come from him.

Jeni saw him striding toward her, his shirt thrown on haphazardly, unbuttoned. The expression on his face was tense and unreadable.

He blushed. "Here. We missed these when we were sorting." Dropping the panties in her lap, he turned to go.

"Oh, I——" A sneeze interrupted her reply.

Brad whirled around. "Are you sick?" he demanded roughly.

"Of course not. I just sneezed."

"I heard you. The important thing is, why?"

"Don't be silly. Everybody sneezes once in a while." Jeni stuffed the panties in her jacket pocket. "I'm fine."

Crouching by her fire, he suggested she spend the night in his dry camper.

Jeni drew a startled breath, then recovered. "Is that a proposition?" she asked, trying to hide the excitement in her voice.

"Of course not!" he nearly roared, snapping to attention. "I'll sleep in your tent."

"Oh." She chewed her lower lip.

Mistaking her disappointment for reticence, he gripped her shoulders, pulling her to her feet. "I won't take no for an answer," he said. "Come on."

Well, she mused, I wanted to spend another night in his camper—but not *alone*. "Brad, I . . ."

"Don't argue," he said flatly. Taking her hand, he led her over the rocks to his camp, opening the camper door. "Do you have everything you need?"

How could she make him stay? Jeni's mind whirled.

Gruffly, Brad repeated his question. "I said, do you need anything from your camp?"

She needed something, all right, Jeni acknowledged. She needed Brad. He was gathering up clean socks, underwear, and a warm sweater.

"Well?"

Why did he seem angry with her? she wondered, hurt by his lack of visible friendliness. "Look, Brad, you don't have to do this," she said.

Did she mean he didn't have to leave? He thought his heart would pound its way out of his chest. "What?"

"I mean, giving me your camper. I told you, I'm not sick. You don't need to coddle me."

So, that was all. Turning on his heel, he stalked out the door. "Good night, Jeni."

What a coward she was! she berated herself. His apparent anger had kept her from saying what she really felt, and now he was gone. She shrugged out of her vest, tossing it on the bench, and kicked off her sneakers. Perched desolately on the edge of his bed, her hand stroked the slick fabric of his sleeping bag. That was it! she realized with a start.

Jeni jerked open the door. "Brad?"

He answered from her tent. "What?"

"I—I've decided I'd rather have my own sleeping bag. Could you bring it in?"

"You've what?"

Oh, dear, she thought, maybe it wasn't such a good idea after all. He'd sounded awfully upset. Well, it was done, so she'd better forge ahead. "Please?"

A rustling inside the tent told her he was complying. Shirtless, he gathered up the copious folds of her red sleeping bag and brought it to her.

"Here."

"You'd better bring it in so I can roll yours up and give it to you. We wouldn't want to drop them and get them dirty." Jeni stuffed her bag into a corner, going through an elaborate ritual of rolling his, and sensing his impatience as well as his imposing physical presence.

Brad shivered. "Hurry up, will you? I'm freezing."

"Close the door," she said, straightening but keeping her back to him. There was no sound from the latch. "I said, close the door," she repeated slowly.

"I don't think I should," Brad said warily.

Still unsure, she refused to look at him. This was all so new, approaching a man like this. If he turned her down, she didn't want to see the look of disgust on his face. "I think you should," she told him, a sensual smoothness to her voice.

The door clicked. Now what? her conscience screamed. He's in here, but you haven't told him why.

"Jeni?" His voice rippled over her like velvet.

"Yes?"

"Can I stay?"

Nodding, she leaned against the bed for support, her legs barely able to support her.

Brad was with her in a split second, holding her up. "Are you all right?" He turned her in his arms, cradling her against the warming expanse of his chest.

"I am now," she whispered, melting into his tender embrace. "Will you stay?"

"If you're sure that's what you want."

"I'm sure." Her arms went around his waist, locking him to her. There was no doubt in her mind he wanted her—she could feel his hard need pressing into her stomach.

"It won't be separate blankets tonight," he warned lovingly.

"I know."

Cradling her flushed cheeks in his palms, he tilted her face up to his. "You're beautiful, Jeni." His lips brushed hers tantalizingly.

Her eyes blazed green fire. "No more raggedy puppy?" she teased.

A low chuckle escaped him. "No more puppy."

"Good," she said, aglow in the ecstasy of his touch, the feel of his body next to hers, "then you won't have to bite me to keep me in line."

Brad laughed. "Don't count on it." His head dipped to her shoulder, then nuzzled her neck, his teeth nipping gently at the sweet flesh.

"Hey!" Giggling, Jeni tried to push him away. "No fair." Wiggling, she fitted her mouth to his neck, sucking roguishly.

He jumped back, clasping the spot. "You stinker. You don't play fair."

"You're absolutely right," Jeni told him, smiling sweetly. "Besides, I'll bet it's been years since you've had a hickey."

"You didn't!" Brad leaned in front of the mirror, examining the red blotch she'd left on his neck. "Why you . . ."

Wide-eyed, she clamped her hands over her mouth, seeing him start for her, then leap across the bed, dragging her with him. Jeni shrieked.

"Shhh. Do you want the park rangers knocking on the door?" Brad shook his head at her, his dark eyes glowing with escalating desire. "No, Kemo Sabe," she whispered sensually. "Come on, bite the silver bullet and kiss me."

"I doubt the Lone Ranger and Tonto had quite this close a relationship," he said. His smile had reached his eyes and they twinkled mischievously.

"We could be Lois Lane and Superman," she suggested.

"Only if *I* get to be Superman," he said, grinning broadly.

"You'll have to convince me you fit the part," Jeni quipped, running her hands over his shoulders and tickling the curly dark hairs on his chest. "Think you're up to it?"

"Honey, I've been 'up' for days because of you. It should be against the law for a woman to do that to a man."

"You don't like women?" she teased. "Seems to me you do."

"That's because you're the woman I like," he confessed. "Believe me, they don't all affect me the way you do."

"Oh? And what about your little ranger friend?"

Brad looked at her with surprise. "You're jealous, aren't you?"

"Absolutely not," she lied.

"Yes, you are, and I love it," he said.

Jeni's voice had become a sultry invitation when she said, "Tell me what else you love, Brad. Tell me how to please you."

She'd meant every word of the provocative statement and he knew it, feeling his desire for her heighten past the point of no return. "Let me show you, honey," he whispered raggedly, reaching for the soft mound of her breast.

As his lips descended to hers, Jeni closed her eyes in

feverish expectation. The kiss deepened, kindling a fire that had been banked for so long she nearly exploded with released longing and need. Her mouth clung to Brad's while she writhed beneath him. Kneading his lips with hers, her fingers wound into his thick hair, pulling him closer.

Jeni couldn't wait for him to remove her sweater. She inched it up under her arms, exposing the thin lace enclosing her straining breasts.

"Oh, Jeni," he moaned.

Squirming beneath his tender attack, she unclasped her bra and removed it.

Brad gasped hoarsely, then took a small pink nipple in his teeth, barely touching the tip with his tongue.

Jeni arched her body in a primitive demand for his. Fingers entwined in his hair, she drew his face to hers, her tongue plunging into his mouth in a thrusting cadence she wordlessly begged him to duplicate in her trembling body.

Lost in the rapture of her abandon, Brad tugged roughly at her sweater, discarded it, and unfastened her jeans.

Lifting her hips, Jeni helped him, then tore at the remaining barrier between them. "Brad, please!" she begged. "I—I need you so."

He stripped quickly, returning to her clinging embrace. "I know, honey, I know," he moaned.

Jeni forced her eyes open. "It's *you* I want," she breathed into the passion-filled atmosphere, "only you. Please—love me."

The moment his body touched the warm welcome she offered, he was lost. With a sharp cry, he took her, as if they had always belonged together.

Gasping, Jeni received him, surprised at the quick jolt of sweet pain that coursed through her. It was almost as if he were the first, she marveled, losing herself in the pleasure-filled sensations he was giving her.

Struggling to maintain control, Brad held himself over her, gazing into the green depths of her misty eyes. "Jeni, are you okay?"

"It's just been a long time, Brad," she whispered. "A very long time."

"There've been no others?" he asked, hardly able to believe a sensuous woman like Jeni had denied herself.

"No. No others," she breathed against the hair on his chest. "In that sense, I guess you're the first."

"I'm glad," he confessed, emotionally overcome. She was beautiful, inside and out. Brad reached for the light switch to hide the depths of his feelings.

Glad for the cover of darkness, Jeni arched toward him again, less inhibited than before. Lifting herself, she twisted and ground against his firm hips, her hands traveling in maddening paths over the glistening flesh of his back and shoulders.

"Oh, Jeni," he confessed. "You drive me crazy!"

She dug her nails into him as a tremor surged through her. "Brad!"

"I know, honey," he gasped, "I know." Increasing his assault on her willing body, he drove harder and harder. "Now, Jeni!"

Jeni could hardly breath as a guttural moan came from the depths of her soul, joining the wild trembling of her exploding passion.

Every muscle in Brad's body tensed, his breathing ceasing for a long, precious moment. Then, with a ragged sigh, he collapsed against her, kissing her hard.

Folding her arms lovingly around him, she rubbed the knotted muscles in his back, a pleased smile on her bruised, love-softened lips.

When Brad had had time to catch his breath, she told him, "Well, you get the part."

He rolled aside and looked quizzically at her profile, dimly outlined against the curtain. "What?"

Jeni smiled sweetly. "You know—faster than a speeding bullet, more powerful than a locomotive . . ."

"Superman."

"Yup. Congratulations."

Brad grinned sheepishly, glad she couldn't see him. "Thanks. Does that mean you liked it?"

"Well . . ." She couldn't resist the chance to tease him. He tensed, starting to pull away. "Hey. Don't leave," she sputtered. "I liked it. I liked it."

"You're sure?"

"Well . . ."

"Jeni," he warned, "don't play with me."

"I thought you liked to play," she taunted, searching boldly, touching him, and feeling his ready response.

"Have a heart, woman," Brad groaned. "At least let me catch my breath."

"I just wanted to prove I liked it. What better way than to ask for a repeat performance?"

"You *do* think I'm Superman, don't you?"

"The man of steel, himself." Jeni was giggling. Reaching for him in a provocative taunt, she rubbed her breasts against his chest.

"Agh! Lady, you're asking for it!"

"Gee, I hope so," she drawled, letting her fingers trace the path of fine hair to below his waist. "That was the idea."

Brad held her close in a possessive, tight embrace. What a woman she was, he thought, grateful to be the one she'd chosen to be with. His. She'd just been his and would be again. And later? Brad pushed his thoughts of the future into the back of his mind.

"Have you rested enough yet?" Jeni asked coquettishly.

"Maybe." Rolling her over, he pinned her to the bed.

"If I doze off in the middle of this, you will wake me, won't you?"

She tried to close her legs, but he was already almost in possession of her pliant warmth. "If you're *that* tired, maybe we should call the whole thing off."

Brad gently eased them together, renewing their oneness. "I don't think so, do you?" he asked very slowly.

She couldn't answer as his intimate invasion took her breath away. Wrapping her legs around him, she urged him closer. Words of love filled her mind and soul; the words she couldn't let herself say. Oh God, she *did* love him, Jeni acknowledged, and it was tearing her apart. What about Timmy? Brad had so thoroughly saturated her thoughts, her feelings, that she'd not even considered the boy.

This is a fling, Jeni, she reminded herself. Don't go making a big deal out of it. She should just be thankful she had tender thoughts for the man with her. How sordid it would seem if she awoke and discovered she hated the guy.

Brad's kisses urged her automatic responses, but her mind was still on Timmy. If he'd been along like she'd planned, this could never have happened. *And,* she wouldn't feel finally alive, she decided thoughtfully. What's wrong with wanting to be a real woman again, in the arms of a real man?

"Superman?" she murmured dreamily.

"Yes, Lois?" he answered.

"Can we go flying again? I really did like it."

"Yes, Lois," Brad whispered, increasing the pressure between her soft thighs. "Let's."

Chapter Five

Whatever embarrassment Jeni had expected to feel in the morning never materialized. It seemed as if they had always been together, and the relaxed, love-filled atmosphere didn't dissipate with the advent of the new day.

She awoke to find herself curled in his arms. "Mmmm."

"Morning, honey." Brad was smiling down at her. With great gentleness, he brushed back her soft curls, tucking her hair behind her ear. "Did you sleep well?"

Jeni felt immersed in his presence. "Umm," she drawled sleepily, "I don't think I slept much."

Brad laughed deeply. "And whose fault was that?"

Stretching, she found a new soreness in her muscles. "Ouch. What did you do to me last night? I'm stiff all over."

"Me? You were the one thrashing all over the bed. It's a wonder we didn't tip the camper over."

Poking him in the ribs, she blushed demurely. "Was I too much for you, Superman?"

"Almost." He kissed her forehead, pulling her closer. "Do you want to get up or stay here all day?"

Jeni tentatively moved her arms and legs, wincing from the aches she found there. "I think we'd better get up while I can still move," she gibed. "I guess I'm out of shape."

He cupped her breast gently. "Feels like a good shape to me."

Feigning disgust, she pushed him away. "Cool it, buster. What makes you think you can take liberties with me?" A smile tugged at the corners of her mouth.

Brad grinned lovingly at her. "Mother warned me about women like you. She said you'd take advantage of me, use my body, then discard me like a worn shoe."

"Mother was a smart lady," Jeni quipped, patting his cheek. Lord, he was attractive. His appeal, just lying there, was enough to turn her heart inside out and rekindle the warm glow in her innermost core. How could she *not* love him?

"Want to go fishing?" she asked, trying for a nonchalant attitude.

"No." Brad could hardly keep himself from grabbing her, then and there, and beginning a replay of their miraculous night. Only her earlier mention of aching muscles stopped him.

"I've only got one more day on my license," she told him, "and I don't want to waste the opportunity."

"Think of the opportunity you'll be wasting if you leave me," he reminded her.

"Oh, I'm not leaving you. You're coming too." She jerked the sleeping bag partway off him. "Rise and shine."

"You have a mean streak a mile wide, O'Brian," he complained pleasantly.

"And don't you forget it," she shot back with a sly smile. "Now, get your clothes on before I weaken and change my mind."

"There's a chance?" His eyebrows raised expectantly.

Struggling to quickly dress, Jeni shook her head. "Nope. I really am stiff and sore all over."

Brad softened. "And *I* really am sorry. Want an aspirin?"

"Is that like saying, take two aspirin and call me in the morning?"

"No. It's like saying, take two aspirin and call me as soon as you feel well enough to mess around some more."

"Ah. The truth comes out." Jeni finished tucking in her shirt tails and zipped her jeans. "Ply me with aspirin and wait, huh?"

Pulling on his pants, Brad stood and placed his hands lightly on her shoulders. "The truth, Jeni, is that I've never experienced anything to compare with our night together. It meant a lot to me. So do you."

His serious demeanor moved her deeply. "It meant the same to me, Brad," she replied softly, knowing it was the truth and terrified to consider farther into the future than the next few days. Her time with Brad was supposed to be transient, a fleeting fancy. Instead, it had made her long for more, for a continuing relationship.

Looking up at him, she saw adoration reflected in his steady gaze. He did realize what they'd found and shared couldn't be permanent, didn't he? Close to telling him, Jeni stopped herself. If doing so destroyed their happy time together, she'd never forgive herself.

Jeni let her fingers lazily trace a big S on his bare chest. "Come on, Superman," she said quietly, "let's go fishing."

Mrs. Andrews at the boat rental desk greeted them warmly. "Morning, folks."

Brad held the lodge door for Jeni, following her into the foyer. "Good morning," he said. "We'd like a boat."

With an understanding smile, the woman asked, "One?"

Jeni nodded. "One." By her quick mental tally she figured she could legally catch five more fish and Brad six, before they reached their limits. "You'd better make that for the whole day," she added.

Taking out a packet of travelers' checks, Brad paid the entire bill, over Jeni's objections.

"Shush, O'Brien. We'll settle up later." His sly wink made Jeni blush when she realized the woman at the rental counter had seen him and looked quickly away, smiling.

"Oh," Brad added, "and a package of marshmallows—make that two packages. O'Brien here eats the bait."

Jeni whopped him playfully on the arm. "Stop telling all my secrets," she retorted.

Handing a small package of marshmallows to each of them, Mrs. Andrews said, "These are on the house. Have a good day, folks."

Brad nodded. Jeni thanked her and popped a soft, white marshmallow in her mouth before following him out the door. He was already getting their gear out of the truck.

"Come on, Jeni. This was your idea. Start carrying," he ordered.

"Fine thing," she complained, lowering her voice. "One little night in the sack and you start telling me what to do."

Brad took a swing at her derriere, connecting with a resounding whack. "You bet. You ordered me around all night and took advantage of my weakened condition. Now, it's my turn."

"Weakened condition!" Too late, she realized she'd nearly shouted, drawing the amused attention of several passers-by.

Brad's shoulders were shaking with silent laughter.

Without waiting for him, she hoisted as much as she could carry and hurried toward the dock. "Morning, Ronnie." She stacked the gear at her feet.

"Morning," the young man said. "I guess I missed seeing you yesterday."

"No. I wasn't here," she explained. "Had to go to Cedar City."

"Oh. Well, I wanted to thank you for rescuing that klutz from the weeds the other day. He was some fisherman, huh?"

Jeni did the only thing she could; she nodded in agreement.

Ronnie started to go on, then spotted Brad. "Oh-oh. Here he comes again. This should be good." The boy tried to squelch an amused expression.

"Ready, O'Brien?" Brad asked pleasantly, handing the boat receipt to Ronnie.

The boy promptly turned a bright pink, apology written all over his flushed face, his eyes pleading with Jeni for understanding.

"Ready," she said smiling. "Come on, Ronnie. Show us which boat is ours."

"Oh—uh—sure," he stammered. Reaching into a shed, he withdrew two floating cushions that doubled as life preservers. "This way."

Jeni stepped into the boat, taking the gear as Brad handed it to her. "Who drives?" she asked him.

"I'll defer to the expert," Brad said, bowing low. "Each of us should do what we do best, don't you think?" His knowing look and bedroom eyes left no doubt as to where he felt his talents lay.

"I love a modest man," Jeni gibed. "Get in."

The motor roared and Jeni steered them clear of the dock area and out onto the lake.

"I think we embarrassed our young friend," Brad observed.

"Uh-huh. He'd just finished telling me what a klutz you were when he realized we were together."

Laughing, Brad said, "I see. No wonder he was doing an imitation of a boiled lobster. Poor kid."

Well, Jeni thought, that was a switch for Brad. He was actually showing compassion for a young person. Of course, Ronnie was nearly an adult. Perhaps that made the difference; smaller children were obviously the ones Brad passionately disliked. Small like Timmy, she added sorrowfully.

"Yoo-hoo," Brad called, waving his arms. "Wake up before you run us aground."

"Sorry." One look told Jeni she was close enough to the right spot to drop anchor. She cut the engine. "Okay. Here we are."

Regarding her seriously, Brad asked if she was all right.

"Sure." Jeni stepped over the rear seat and placed herself next to him. "Even better, now."

When both lines were in the water, Brad encouraged her to lie down with her head in his lap. The boat tilted crazily until they'd found the center of balance.

He stroked her hair. "Think we could make love in one of these unstable rocking chairs?"

Jeni smiled up at him. "Probably not. Besides, what if we got a bite while we were otherwise occupied?" She giggled. "That might be very interesting."

An hour later, Brad approached the subject again. "Well, O'Brien, we haven't had so much as a nibble. See what a waste it was to postpone making love?"

Sighing, she sat up and reeled in her untouched bait. "If you don't stop talking like that, I'm going to go mad before the day's over."

"You mean it sounds good to you?" he taunted. "I'd begun to think *you* were the one made of steel."

"Hardly." Changing bait, she cast again. "Did we remember to stow all the gear back in camp?"

"I think so. Why?"

Jeni pointed to the southern sky. "Looks like The Breaks is getting wet again."

Dark, heavy clouds were crowding the horizon. "It also looks like it may be coming this way," he said cautiously.

"Oh, I doubt——" A strong strike brought Jeni to her feet. "I've got one! About time, too," she shouted. "Get the net!"

Jeni had caught three fish and Brad two by the time the first lightning was visible. The lake surface had developed a dangerous chop and the wind was moving them shoreward in spite of their anchors.

Brad reeled in his line and started to hoist the bow anchor.

"What are you doing?" she shrieked. "They're finally biting!"

"And this is a metal boat, lady," Brad said firmly. "We're going in."

"No!"

"Yes. I may be a novice at fishing, but I'm no fool. No one in his right mind would stay out here in this storm."

She made a face at him.

"Look around you, Jeni. Where is everybody?"

Brad was right, she had to admit. Reeling in, she helped him with the stern anchor, then started the motor. Opening the throttle full bore, she headed the small boat into the howling wind.

At first their progress was fair, but as the storm built, the tiny craft hardly moved.

"Jeni!" Shouting to be heard above the roar of the storm, Brad pointed to the closer banks. "We'd better get ashore."

She nodded, swinging in a wide arc to prevent capsizing in the large waves. With the wind at their backs, they fairly flew. Jeni released the tilt lever on the motor and raised the prop as the boat beached itself.

Brad was over the bow in seconds, tugging the rest of the hull out of the water. Tremendous drops of rain had begun to pelt them. "Come on!" He took her hand and lifted her onto the sand. "Let's make a run for it."

"Where? There's nothing on this side of the lake." It was getting harder and harder to see as the rain increased. Was Brad out of his mind? she wondered. There were no buildings where he was leading her, only cliffs.

"Duck," he called, dragging her down with him.

Suddenly, they were dry and sheltered. Jeni looked around in wonder. It wasn't exactly a cave, she decided, staring at the rock overhang. Still, it was close. "How did you . . . ?"

Brad was shaking off the water. "I had time to spot this place while you were busy navigating. It's not plush, but it sure beats drowning." He'd settled himself on the hard floor, leaning against a sloping wall. "Come here, O'Brien."

"Still giving orders, I see," she observed, standing her ground.

"How about, please come here and I'll make love to you?"

Jeni sank to her knees beside him, gently caressing his face. "Much better," she whispered. "Do you think we're safe here?"

"Unless the U.S. Coast Guard patrols Panguitch Lake," he said quietly.

"I don't think they do."

"Neither do I." Brad reached under her arms and shifted her so she straddled his lap.

Putting her hands on his shoulders, Jeni let her fingers creep around his neck and tangle in his damp hair. "Good," she said breathlessly, "good."

Brad drew her closer, his hands beneath her jacket. He wanted to tell her how he felt, wanted to speak of love, of the fathomless depths of his feelings for her, but he stopped himself. What right did he have to come along and disrupt her life, her future plans? The rights of a lover? Perhaps. And suppose he did tell her he loved her? He was a man without a career, without a stable future. What could he offer her that she didn't already have in abundance? Only a moment of pleasure, he concluded, only a body that ached to possess her with a soul-deep desire he'd never before encountered.

Settling herself into his embrace, Jeni brought her lips slowly down to his. Their first tentative touch escalated like the storm, becoming a raging tempest in moments. Jeni groaned with the agony of wanting, pressing herself to his body in abandon. "Brad," she gasped against his mouth.

"Oh, Jeni, my love, my beautiful love, I need you so." He reached for the snap on her jeans and found her hand already there, pushing away the interfering denim. She slid her clothing off and returned to her perch on his lap, once again seeking the temporary solace of his kiss.

Brad's hands caressed the warm roundness of her hips, slipping up under her shirt to tease her oversensitized breasts.

"Oh, Brad!" she moaned, "I need you, too." Unbuttoning her shirt, she freed herself totally to his exploration, watching in awe as his mouth closed around one rosy nipple, then the other.

His own need strained beneath his clothing. Jeni's hands found and caressed his poorly hidden desire, her fingers pulling at the zipper.

Brad helped her, then returned to her breasts, kissing them languorously, yet passionately.

Jeni was beside herself with longing. Reaching lower, she found him, freed him, and settled herself possessively over him, hearing his sharp intake of breath as she did so.

Closing his eyes, he rolled his head back and grasped her hips, thrusting upward in a sensual intensity that brought a cry of pleasure to her lips. "Not so fast, honey," he urged. "Take your time."

But Jeni didn't want to wait. She wanted him *now*. It was almost more than she could bear. "Brad, please!" she begged, beginning a slow, rocking motion. "Please!"

He'd intended to fight her, to make the moment last for both of them, but Jeni's building cadence was carrying him along in an avalanche of feeling. She was gripping him frantically, her breasts dancing before him through the open folds of her shirt. His lips sought one nipple, closing around it and pulling it into his mouth in the same way she was working her magic on him.

With a guttural cry, Jeni writhed against him, holding his head to her breast.

Brad's hands were on her hips, helping her keep up the primitive rhythm till she pierced the storm with sharp screams of delight, her whole body seized in the ultimate convulsion. His own flesh answered and he joined her, suspended for a moment between the storm outside and the storm in his own soul. Then Brad felt her go limp and sag against him.

"Jeni," he soothed. "Oh, Jeni."

Breathing hard, she held on to him like a drowning person to a life preserver. Tears misted her eyes. Every time with Brad was more beautiful, more exciting. And each time she felt more of a loss when it was over. She was like a lemming, Jeni brooded, driven, running toward the steep cliffs to plunge into the sea and power less to stop herself.

"Brad, I . . ."

Tenderly, he kissed the top of her head. "Shhh. Rest a bit, then we'll talk." Jeni had been like a woman possessed, he mused, holding her closer. He'd never seen anyone react quite the way she had. It was almost as i she were afraid he'd somehow disappear or leave her. Stroking her, he noticed she was getting chilly. "Sit up, honey, and get dressed before you do catch a cold."

"No." She was clinging tightly to him. "Just hold me."

"I will, Jeni, I will. But first put your clothes back on. Then I'll hold you as long as you like. I promise."

Hesitantly, she eased herself off him and replaced her clothing. She couldn't look him in the eye. What must he think of her, practically attacking him and carrying on like she had? She'd never acted that way before. Never. Brad must think she was a maniac.

Holding out his arms, he urged her to return. "Come here, honey."

Jeni snuggled next to him, her cheek on his chest.

"Can I tell you something?" he asked quietly.

She nodded, her movement barely perceptible.

"I, uh," Brad cleared his throat, "I've never been loved quite like that before. You were really something."

Fresh tears slid out of Jeni's eyes. "I—I'm sorry if I embarrassed you," she stammered weakly.

He tilted her face up to him, wiping the tears from her cheeks. "You've missed the point, O'Brien," he teased amiably. "I loved it."

She sniffed. "You did?"

"Uh-huh. I did."

"And you're not thinking bad things about me?"

"No-o-o," he emphasized. "As a matter of fact, I was thinking about asking you to spend the rest of your vacation with me. How much more time do you have?"

Jeni did some quick calculation. "Eight days, plus one for the drive home." She stared at him. "Are you serious?"

"Very. I don't see why we should go from day to day wondering if we'll see each other when we can set up the whole thing and plan some fun side trips. Do you?"

"No, I don't," she replied happily.

"Then it's a deal?"

"A deal," she said hurriedly. "I'd love it."

Brad kissed her lightly. "I don't suppose we need to shake on it to seal the bargain, do we?"

"I have a better idea," Jeni drawled, snaking her hand under his shirt.

"I'll bet you do," Brad chuckled. "O'Brien, I have the feeling I'm going to remember this vacation for a long time to come."

"So am I," she sighed wistfully. "So am I."

The afternoon passed in a blur of ecstasy, promised and fulfilled.

Jeni dug into her jacket pocket, extracting a small plastic bag. "Marshmallow?" She held the bag up to Brad.

"Thanks. I guess this is lunch."

"I guess." She checked her watch and, glancing outside, saw that the weather was clearing. "If we don't start back soon, they're liable to come looking for us."

Brad agreed. "I suppose." He took a deep breath, releasing it as a sigh. "You never told me where you lived, Jeni. Does it really take you a whole day to drive home?" He was counting the minutes they had left to be together.

"Los Angeles, basically. I live in the suburbs, but that's the area. What about you?" she asked in return. "You never said where you were from, either."

"Nebraska."

"Nebraska!" she exclaimed. "And you never learned to get along in the wilds?"

Brad laughed aloud. "You make it sound like the end of civilization. Omaha's a big city."

"And you live there?"

"I did." He got to his feet, dusting himself off. "I don't live anywhere anymore."

A puzzled look crossed her face. "You what?"

Slipping his hands in his pockets, Brad faced her

squarely. "You've been sleeping in my house," he said. "All my worldly possessions are now stowed in that camper."

"But don't you plan to go back? I mean, your family, your friends . . .?"

"Nope. Not for a while, anyway. I told you I was searching for a new career, a new place. The Indian boy in the wilderness, remember? I'd been on the road nearly a week when I got up the nerve to really try camping. That's where you came in."

She was strangely quiet. "I see." How could anyone abandon a career, a home and family, and take off across country with no specific plan or purpose? What was he running from?

"Jeni?" Brad's arm was around her shoulders.

Sagging against him, she circled his waist. "Hmmm?"

"Shall we take in Bryce Canyon or Zion National Park, tomorrow? I hear they're both beautiful."

Jeni remembered vaguely that neither place was far from Cedar Breaks. "Sure."

He hugged her closer. "I want to share everything with you, Jeni, for as long as you'll have me."

Could he feel her heart begin to thud? she wondered. Of course, he'd only meant during her vacation. It was just that he'd sounded so—so permanent. How permanent can we get in eight days? she asked herself sarcastically. About as lasting as a blazing campfire, hot and flaming for a short while, then nothing more than ashes, no longer warm, with no chance of rekindling.

Well, she reasoned, eight days was eight days. If that was all the time they had, she'd be a real fool to waste it dwelling on the distant future. She kissed him quickly. "Come on, Superman. I'll race you to the boat."

He let her win, then pushed the boat into the lake and vaulted in. "Ready." Joining her on the rear seat, Brad touched her hair, brushing silky strands away from her face. Her cheeks were flushed from the outdoors, her eyes still aglow from their private afternoon. "How about letting me take you out to dinner?" he said loudly over the roar of the motor. "They tell me the food's great in Brian Head."

"The ski resort?"

Brad nodded. "There's a little Mexican restaurant there that's open all year."

She smoothed her hair. "I don't know. I feel like I've spent the day rolling around in a cave, or something. I'm pretty grubby."

"You look perfect to me," he said, smiling slightly, "but if it bothers you, why don't you take a shower at the lodge?"

"Do they do that? I mean, could I?"

"Sure." Brad seemed rather pleased with himself. "And you'll have clean clothes because I put your suitcase in the truck before we left camp."

"You've thought of everything, haven't you?"

"I try."

"And you'd planned to ask me out to dinner tonight?" She saw him shrug noncommittally, a wide grin spreading across his handsome face. "I suppose you'd planned our little rendezvous, too."

"As a matter of fact, no," he said. "I was still trying to figure out how we could make love in this blasted boat when the storm took care of the problem."

Jeni laughed. "Oh, you were, were you?"

He lunged toward her, grabbing her awkwardly while the boat zig-zagged recklessly through the water. "Do I need to prove it?"

"No. No!" she squealed. "Stop it. You'll wreck us both!"

Releasing her, he leaned away. The wreck was him, Brad thought cynically, his emotional state. Jeni had turned his whole world inside out and he didn't know what would come of it. He felt like a train on a collision course with another speeding locomotive on the same track. He didn't know whether they'd survive the outcome, but it had to be one hell of a crash.

They walked up the dock together, stowed their gear, and took their catch to the lodge to be frozen. Jeni was rummaging for clean clothes when Brad returned with a key. She was incredulous. "You got a room? What's the matter with just using the bath house?"

His reaction was almost comical.

"Brad," she accused, "you're blushing."

Half his mouth smiled. "Maybe, a little. I thought, this way, we could clean up together." The other half of his face joined the smile. "After all, I did get you dirty."

"With a little help from me," she confessed. "I can't imagine what Mrs. Andrews is going to think."

"I can," Brad said. "She looked at me like a coach getting a team ready for the big game." He proceeded to quote, " 'There's shampoo in the medicine chest, ice cubes in a machine in the hall, extra towels behind the bathroom door, and if you need anything else . . .' "

"Oh, Brad." Jeni was laughing heartily.

"Think we'll need anything else?"

Putting her arms around his waist, she hugged him close. "All I need is warm water, shampoo, and *you*, you big lug." She gave him a quick kiss. "Which way to the room?"

Swinging her suitcase off the ground, Brad said, "I thought you'd *never* ask," and led her up the stairs.

The room was rustically charming, totally in keeping with the area, and Jeni immediately loved it. She poked her head into the large, delicately floral-papered bathroom. "Wow. There's enough room in here for . . ." Her eyes darted furtively to Brad.

"That's what our landlady said."

"She didn't!" Jeni was mortified.

He chuckled. "No, she didn't, but it sounds like a great idea." Brad glanced at the telephone on the nightstand. "Maybe we should phone the ranger station up at The Breaks and explain that we won't be back tonight. That way, they won't tow our stuff away or worry about your being lost."

"Let's not tell them where we *really* are, okay?"

"Embarrassed?"

"A little," she said honestly. "I don't usually . . ."

"I know," Brad assured her seriously. "If you don't want to stay, we don't have to."

Jeni was adamant. "No. I *do* want to." She thought for a moment. "You know, I should call my sister, too. I'd told her she could reach me at Cedar Breaks and I don't want her to worry. Then I can tell her I'll be at Bryce or Zion tomorrow, too."

"Fine. Go ahead."

She'd crossed the colorful braided rug and wrapped him in another embrace. "That can wait till later. It's earlier in California, anyway, and we have a long, hot shower to take."

"We?" he asked, pretending astonishment. "Why, O'Brien!"

"We, Superman. Let's see if you're still made of steel, shall we?" She'd unbuttoned and eased off his shirt while she was talking.

"In that case, suppose we see what *you're* made of, O'Brien." His hands gently and expertly stripped her, brushing her off. "Um. You are kind of sandy," he observed.

Jeni made a silly face at him. "Maybe you should phone The Breaks now, before we get too involved, if you know what I mean. I'll go turn on the shower and get the water warmed up for you."

Shrugging out of the rest of his clothes, Brad sat on the edge of the quilt covering the large, inviting bed and put through the call. When he entered the bathroom, Jeni was already lathering her hair.

"Did they say it was okay?" Soapy water dripping down her forehead made her squeeze her eyes tightly closed. Why didn't he answer? she wondered. "Brad?"

"I'm here, honey." Slowly, he drew aside the plastic curtain and joined her.

Jeni put out her hands, finding and touching him. "So I see."

Brad rinsed himself thoroughly, then pulled her into a tight embrace.

"Brad, wait. Let me get this soap off first." She let the water cascade through her clean hair, then rinsed her eyes, turning to him. The look on his face told her something was wrong.

"What is it? Did a tree fall on my car, or what?" Her feeble attempt at humor fell flat. "Brad?"

"Your sister's name is Linda, isn't it?"

"Yes." Jeni wracked her brain to remember when she'd told him that. She hadn't. "How did you know?"

"I called the ranger station," he said slowly. "They had a message for you from Linda. You're to phone her immediately."

The possibilities crowded in on Jeni. "Did they say why?"

Brad kissed her briefly under the rushing water. "No. Don't you know?"

"I . . ." There was only one reason why Linda would leave an urgent message. Timmy must be finally in her custody.

"Jeni, talk to me. What's going on?"

She held him close, listening to his strong heartbeat pound in her ears. It was still early. Putting off the call would buy a little more precious time together. She was entitled to that, damn it.

"It can't be much," she lied unconvincingly. "Don't worry. I'll phone her later, like I'd planned."

Brad didn't believe a word. *Everything* was wrong. Jeni was strung as tight as a ten-pound-test fishing line with a hundred-pound shark on the other end. He found himself stiffly unresponsive when she reached up to kiss him. "Are you finished showering?" he asked.

Jeni didn't want to leave the bath. What she did want was for Brad to hold her, love her, and take away the empty feeling beginning to gnaw at her. His facial expression and stance told her it was futile. There was no use trying, so she stepped out onto the mat.

Wrapping a fluffy white towel around her hair, she proceeded to dry herself with another.

"Brad," she said quietly, "don't worry so much. I told you, it was nothing."

Anger blazed in his eyes. "Yes, you did, didn't you? You're awfully sure of that when you haven't talked to Linda yet." He rubbed himself dry with furious speed. "I *thought* we trusted each other."

"We do!" Jeni insisted. "I trust you, Brad."

"Oh?" he continued sarcastically. "Then why are you lying to me?"

"I . . ." Tears clouded her eyes. "I just didn't want anything to spoil our time together, that's all."

"And what would do that?" he questioned skeptically. "All you have to do is phone your sister, take care of whatever the problem is, and we can go out to dinner. Right?" When she didn't answer, he pressed, "Well, isn't that right?"

Jeni's voice was low and unsteady. Pulling on clean clothes, she answered him, "I guess so." How could she make that call? Her hands were shaking so badly she could hardly dress herself. Her stomach churned. They'd planned to spend the time with each other. Now, all that was over before it had really begun.

Sinking to the edge of the bed, Jeni looked imploringly at Brad. "Can't we go to dinner first? I can call Linda when we get back."

Brad stopped combing his hair, the comb poised in midair. "Why?"

"I just thought . . ."

He was adamant. "Get it over with. We may be late getting in and you don't want to wake her up and scare her to death." Darkly piercing, his eyes followed Jeni's every move as she lifted the receiver, asked for an outside line, and dialed.

All her hopes that no one would answer were dashed on the third ring.

"Hello?"

"Linda? It's Jeni."

The older woman bubbled with excitement. "It's gone through, Jen! I got the word yesterday. Your lawyer called and said the custody papers were on his desk."

"That's great, Linda," Jeni told her, her voice close to breaking.

Linda sensed the crackling emotion in her sister's response, mistaking it for a reaction of joy and relief. "Get a grip on yourself, little sister," she said, "I've got a bus ticket for Tim to St. George. He's all packed and rarin' to go. Can you meet him—let's see—in about fourteen hours? That's nine A.M. our time and . . ."

"Ten o'clock here," Jeni muttered. Taking a deep breath, she pulled herself together, her sense of responsibility overriding the temporary insanity Brad had fostered in her. "Sure. From Cedar Breaks to St. George is only a couple of hours, round-trip. Tell him I'll start out early and not to worry. I'll be there." Her mood was beginning to lighten. This was what she'd waited and hoped and prayed for for so very long. How could she not feel some elation?

"Why don't you tell him yourself?" Linda asked. "He's right here."

The small voice said, tentatively, "Hello?"

Jeni's heart went out to the lost sounding, frail little boy. "Timmy, honey! Hi. I've missed you."

Brad had leaned back against the mahogany dresser, his arms folded defensively across his chest. He'd watched Jeni go from depression to exuberance in a matter of minutes. The boy was coming. That discovery didn't surprise Brad much. Jeni's strange reaction to the message to phone Linda had told him something was up, but why did she want to hide it? he wondered. Why not simply tell him the truth?

Timmy had told Jeni all about his new clothes before Linda interrupted, instructed him gently to say goodbye, and took the receiver. "Listen, Jen, this is costing you a fortune. You'll see Tim in St. George tomorrow. Take care."

"You're right, Linda, and—" she paused to control her emotions—"thanks."

Linda was not unmoved when she replied, "No problem. Love ya."

Sitting immobile on the edge of the bed after replacing the phone, Jeni barely noticed Brad's quiet approach.

He eased himself down beside her. "Timmy?"

Staring blankly at him, Jeni nodded. Everything was changed, now. She was no longer a free spirit who could flit around all over the countryside with an attractive man whenever she felt like it. She had responsibilities. She had Timmy. "I have to leave."

"Now? What about dinner?" Brad asked, sensing the futility of arguing with her.

Jeni jumped to her feet, pacing the floor. "I have to get my camp ready and check the car for the trip down to St. George, and I'll have to get extra groceries, and—and be ready to start for the city by eight A.M."

"You're really excited about this, aren't you?" he asked sadly.

"Of course," she insisted, her nervousness growing. "This is what I've fought for, waited for, for nearly a year."

"And you *knew* when I told you Linda had tried to reach you, didn't you?"

Chagrined, Jeni answered truthfully. "Yes. At least, I suspected."

"But you couldn't tell me?" Brad thrust his hands in his pockets, watching her vigorously towel-dry her hair, and said no more.

Hiding behind the damp folds of the towel, Jeni was glad he hadn't insisted she answer. What good would it do? The man hated children and Timmy was going to be a part of her life from now on. The poor kid had had enough problems in his nine years to last a lifetime. The last thing he needed was for his new mother to saddle him with someone like Brad, even if she loved the man. The thought echoed through her mind—she *loved* the man.

And what did *she* want? her subconscious screamed. Stubbornly, Jeni fought her personal yearnings while her heart cried for Brad and what had been such a perfect few days. She shouldn't have let herself plan those eight days with him, she reasoned; then her disappointment and sense of loss wouldn't have been so great. Oh yeah? her mind shot back. Who says? You'll remember Brad Carey for the rest of your life, Jeni O'Brien, and there's no use denying it.

Chapter Six

❧

Jeni was so wrapped up in her turbulent thoughts, she hardly saw any of the magnificent scenery on the way back to camp. Aspen and spruce forest became broad expanses of flower-filled alpine meadows as they climbed; eight, nine, ten thousand feet.

When Brad backed his truck into his campsite, he turned off the ignition and leaned on the steering wheel "Last chance for dinner."

"No, thanks." She softened toward him. A clean break was the best, she'd decided during the drive home. With her senses dulled by her overwhelming responsibilities, Jeni hadn't stopped to analyze what effect it might have on her personally, she only knew she had to stand firm.

"Can I help you get your camp ready?" Brad asked.

"No." Jeni had opened the door. "I can handle i alone." Slamming the door, she leaned through the oper window. "If you could unload all my things, though, I'c appreciate it."

Brad watched her walk away. So, he thought, that wa that. At least she'd spared him the embarrassment of ask ing her to stay the night with him and being turnee down. He drove his fist hard against the wheel, ther withdrew into deep concentration. Suppose she hadn' meant a final break? Suppose she only wanted to rest ane be ready for the kid? It would be all right to offer to drive her to St. George, wouldn't it?

Toting her suitcase and fishing gear, Brad stepped over the rocks. Night was approaching and Jeni's lantern glowed on the end of the table while she busily sorted and repacked her things.

"Here you are."

Not looking up, she said, "Thanks. Pile it on the table, will you?"

"Jeni?" he said hesitantly. "I could drive you."

She couldn't let that happen. "No. No!"

Resting one booted foot on the bench, Brad asked, "Why not? I thought we——"

"There is no more *we*, Brad," she snapped. "There can't be."

Shrugging his shoulders, he said, "I see."

He took it with such calm that Jeni wanted to scream and beat her fists against his chest. Didn't he care?

Standing quietly, he faced her, his eyes searching hers for any sign of remorse. Finding none, he turned to go.

"Brad?" Jeni's voice quavered unmistakably.

He froze, his back still toward her. "Yes?"

"I—it was good," she said in a near whisper. "I'll never forget you." Tears had gathered in her eyes, the lantern light making them glisten, but Brad never turned, never saw them.

After interminable seconds, he continued making his way back to his own campsite, a droop to his otherwise broad shoulders the only outward sign he'd been affected by her words. The door to his camper slammed.

Terrific, he thought with rancor. He'd found a beautiful, intelligent, sexy woman and some kid comes along and takes her away from him. It seemed like kids would always be his nemesis. An important truth nudged his consciousness and Brad was finally forced to acknowledge it; he didn't hate youngsters. He never really had.

They'd been a part of a trying time in his life, that was all. His sense of fairness made him admit that was the only real problem, but he'd fallen into the habit of expressing an active dislike of all children and it was a hard habit to break.

Brad's eyes widened. Could Jeni be protecting Timmy from him? Surely, she'd know he . . . but why should she? Thinking back, Brad remembered his caustic remarks about kids. It hadn't mattered then. But now . . . If he stayed and won over the boy, maybe the mother would . . . What, Carey? he asked himself seriously. What were his *intentions?* Did he really want a ready-made family? The lady was superb in bed, but was that enough? Or was he ready to tell her he *loved* her?

His hands clenched into tight fists. He had more sense than to fall for a stranger he'd only known a few short days, didn't he? No, he decided, it wasn't really love, he was simply feeling the sting of her rejection, that was all. It had developed into a tangible, physical ache and a feeling of malaise only because Jeni had reneged on dinner and left him unfed and hungry.

He stalked out into the dark night, rummaging in his ice chest in search of a quick snack to assuage his hunger, but found nothing that appealed to him. He'd spent nearly every meal with Jeni since arriving in Cedar Breaks. It seemed unnatural to eat alone. Looking up, he found her watching him and stood motionless, returning her unreadable stare.

In the dark, she could barely see him. Only the sounds in his camp had made her glance over. She could have recognized his outline from among a thousand others the way he moved, his form, the aura that was Brad, and Brad alone.

Jeni wanted to run to him and throw herself into his arms, somehow take them back a day in time to the marvelous discovery of each other's innermost wants and needs, but her feet were rooted where she stood. Mesmerized by his dark stare, she could only watch and wait for him to make the first move. Oh, God, she prayed silently, why doesn't he come to me? Does he hate me for calling it off between us?

Then she had a thought that tore at her heart. Suppose Brad was relieved to be rid of her? Her pulse sped erratically. Brad was moving. Was he . . . ?

Slamming closed the lid on the ice chest, he strode stiffly to his camper. In seconds, he'd switched off the lights.

Well, Jeni admitted, that was that. It had been her decision to break the relationship off before Tim arrived, and she'd stick with it. Unreasonable anger seethed within her. Brad hadn't even cared enough to argue. He could at least have put up a fight. If she'd mattered to him, he would have. It seemed that she was only a tumble in the hay to him, a romp in the sack, a . . . Lurid scenes and phrases bombarded her mind. Damn him. Damn him! she cursed furiously. And I thought he was so special, so wonderful. Hah!

Suddenly, Jeni found herself crying uncontrollably. Burying her face in her hands she tried to still the racking sobs. Blurry-eyed, she locked her car, turned off her lantern, and crawled into her tent, gasping in a continuing effort at control. It was no use.

Jeni realized she hadn't known what lonely was, before. Climbing into her sleeping bag, she zipped herself into the warm cocoon. Horrible grief washed over her, and she let it all out, smothering her desperate, shaking sobs in the padded fabric till she felt she couldn't cry another tear.

This pain couldn't last, she agonized. It wouldn't hurt so much in the morning, and when Timmy got here . . . New tears forced themselves past her weakened defenses. Why did she feel so guilty every time Timmy came to mind? she wondered dully, wiping her eyes with the backs of her hands. She wanted him, didn't she? *Didn't she?*

Shockingly, Jeni realized she was frightened. Not only was the custody of Timmy new, but so was her feeling for Brad. The whole mess was overloading her capacity to deal with the difficulties life was throwing at her.

Taking a shuddering breath, Jeni closed her eyes. She'd feel better in the morning, she assured herself. Everything would fit into place, given time. If not, she'd make it fit. She had to.

Exhausting herself with tears gave Jeni one thing she desperately needed—a good night's sleep. And she honestly *did* feel better the next morning.

Dressing quickly, she layered her clothes so as to be ready for the differences in temperature, first in Cedar City, then St. George. Utah was full of surprises if you weren't prepared ahead of time, and driving in a matter of hours from the desert to the snow could be a shock.

By the time she'd reached Cedar City, she was ready to admit to a hunger for breakfast. Jeni checked her watch to see that she was early. Stopping to eat wouldn't make her late, but she couldn't do it. The gnawing fear of Timmy getting off that bus and not finding her there was overpowering.

Grabbing a quick coffee-to-go, she balanced the steaming Styrofoam cup and entered the highway. Pines became scrub growth along the four-lane road and the sun warmed the new day with the brilliance of clear air.

Jeni rolled down her window, letting the wind toss her thick hair behind her. She glanced at her reflection in the rear-view mirror. Large, circular sunglasses hid the puffiness under her eyes, the only visible remnant of her tearful night. Thoughts of her explosive emotional state brought memories of Brad, but that would never do

Restlessly, she switched on the radio, searching for the St. George station she knew she could get from the northern highway, finding the signal just in time to hear a poignant love song. Disgusted, she flicked off the music, giving up her futile fight against thoughts of Brad Carey.

In a way, she felt sorry for him. Timmy's coming had been a total surprise to him. Considering the fact that all their wonderful plans had been upset, he'd actually taken it extremely well.

He'd been unable to hide the pain he felt when she'd told him there could be nothing more between them, and new tears pooled in her eyes at the thought. It was for the best, she insisted, over and over. He had no claim on her, nor she on him. A handsome, intelligent man like Brad could find dozens of women who'd fall all over themselves to belong to him. God, that realization hurt, she agonized. But what could she do? Circumstances had dictated the outcome of their relationship as surely as if they'd been following a script for a play. What choice did the actors in the drama have? None. "I did the only thing I could," she exclaimed, gripping the wheel. "The *only* thing I could."

Timmy looked tired when he came down the bus steps. His dark hair had once been neatly slicked down, Jeni could see, but sleeping on the bus had mussed it into an adorably casual mop.

"Timmy! Over here."

A look of immense relief replaced the almost frightened expression on his face. In moments, he'd run to Jeni.

She held open her arms, crouching down, and waited to welcome him.

The boy stopped several feet from her embrace, not entering the circle of her arms.

"Timmy?" Jeni's shoulders sagged.

Extending his hand, he waited for her to shake it.

"Oh," she said, understanding but disappointed. "Hello." She shook the small hand, then rose to her feet, eyeing the blue duffel bag Tim had dragged behind him. "Is that all you brought?"

He nodded. "New clothes."

"The ones you told me about?" Jeni asked, trying to draw him out.

Timmy's attention was on a candy machine in the depot. "I'm hungry."

He must be, she thought, after all those hours on the bus. "I could use some breakfast, too, Timmy," she said pleasantly. "Let's go find a restaurant." When she looked down, he was gone.

Standing in front of the candy machine, he said loudly, "I like M&Ms."

Jenni relented. The poor kid had probably had darned little opportunity to satisfy his wants the way other children did. She dug in her purse for change, gratified at Timmy's adoring smile. The package of candy tumbled into the slot. "There," she said, pleased at having had a chance to do it for him. "Now, how about breakfast?"

"I like the peanut ones, too," he added with sugary sweetness. "I can eat *two* packs of those."

Jeni laughed, charmed by his innocent candor. "Oh, you can, can you?"

Nodding vigorously, Timmy flashed her a pleading look. "Please?" Beaming victoriously when she gave in, the boy stuffed the candy into his pockets.

"Now, can we have breakfast?" Jeni asked, laughing at his happy smile. There were several nice coffee shops in St. George and she was looking forward to a leisurely meal before the drive back. "How about pancakes and sausage?" she asked. "Or maybe an egg?"

Tim began to pout. "I only like hamburgers," he

insisted. "I want a hamburger—with cheese and lots of pickles."

Well, she supposed, the coffee shops would serve him a burger while she ate a regular breakfast. "Okay."

Driving along the crowded main street, Jeni tried to choose a restaurant and still carefully navigate the busy thoroughfare. She pulled up at the curb in front of a cafe, locked her door, and went around the car to secure the passenger door.

"Over there!" Timmy shouted, pointing to a drive-through quick food stand. "I want to eat over there." When Jeni hesitated, he added, "You promised!"

Jeni grasped his hand, sighing. Well, what difference did it really make? And if it pleased Timmy . . .

"Okay. Get back in the car," she told him. After all, she rationalized, the boy needed to feel like he was an important part of her family. Once she'd won him over and gained his trust, there'd be plenty of time to teach him concern for others' wants and needs. Right now, giving in to him seemed best.

Letting Tim order whatever he wanted, Jeni settled on a hamburger and a Coke for herself. Her new son ordered two cheeseburgers, fries, a large Coke, and a brownie.

"Good grief, Tim," she marveled, hoping he wouldn't make himself sick, "are you positive you can eat all that?"

"Sure. It's good—and I'm almost nine." As if to prove his capacity and age as well, he quickly polished off the first cheeseburger.

Wiping her hands, Jeni disposed of her trash. "Can you manage to eat while I drive?" she asked. "I'd like to get back up the mountain."

Tim nodded, his mouth too full to talk.

She watched him out of the corner of her eye until she was satisfied he had control of the situation. It took him nearly the whole trip, but he ate everything she'd bought him. Jeni smiled to herself. It felt good to provide for Timmy, to have someone who needed her.

The last few pieces of candy took him a long time to swallow, she noticed, making a mental note to forestall his attempts to gorge himself. It was understandable that he'd pack away lots of food once the supply was unlimited. She'd simply have to explain to him he no longer had to worry about where his next meal was coming from. As he'd said, he was nearly nine years old. He'd understand.

Pulling into Cedar Breaks campground, Jeni noted with a lump in her throat that Brad's truck was gone, his campsite cleaned. Was he coming back? she wondered, or had he moved on, a nomad on wheels.

She reached over, patting Timmy on the leg. "We're here." This was what she'd waited for, her chance to show him the whole world wasn't made up of foul air, dirty alleys, and roving gangs. His expression seemed blank when she'd expected excitement.

Jeni parked in her campsite. "Come on. I'll show you around," she told Timmy. "First of all, the restrooms are over there."

Tim started in that direction.

"Want me to go with you?" Jeni asked.

"Nope."

Watching his small figure go down the narrow path, Jeni found her emotions overflowing with love for her young future son. He'd had a rough start, but that was all behind him now. In no time he'd forget the streets, the hard-bitten attitudes of his brother Alex's cronies, the running away—all the negative aspects his earlier life had held. Alex had been right when he'd asked her to intervene. Timmy wasn't too far gone; there was time.

The sound of a truck engine disturbed her thoughts. Glancing in the direction of the noise, she jumped, her pulse growing rapid. Brad was back.

Parking, he climbed out and came toward her. "Hi."

"Hi." Jeni fought to sound casual, stuffing her trembling hands in her jacket pockets. "I thought you'd gone." She cocked her head in the direction of his empty camp.

"I had." Brad put one foot on the picnic bench. "Where's the boy?"

"In the bathroom." Jeni paused. "Brad, I think you'd better leave before he gets back. He's still getting adjusted to me."

"I thought you'd known him for some time."

"I have, but this is different. I was only his big brother's parole officer before. Now, I have legal custody."

Leaning his elbow on one knee, Brad inquired further. "The adoption isn't final?"

She shook her head. "No. Custody comes first. Then we'll be visited, as a family, by the social workers. There's a lot to it, but it'll all come together. I just couldn't bring Timmy with me till I got clearance to give me custody."

"I see." Brad gestured toward the restroom complex. "That him?"

"Yes," she said anxiously. "Please, Brad . . ."

He stepped over the rocks and began unloading his gear while he watched Jeni greeting Timmy. A cute little kid, Brad decided. Kind of reminded him of himself, he noticed with a smile. Raised voices in Jeni's camp made it easy for him to overhear without trying. As a matter of fact, he couldn't have *helped* hearing, and he didn't like the gist of the conversation one bit.

Tim's shrill whine carried easily. "I am *too* hungry!"

"Timmy," Jeni said, trying to remain firm but gentle, "you've just finished the last of your candy. Be sensible."

"But, I'm hungry!"

"There's plenty, Tim," she told him. "Here. Look."

Lifting the lid on her ice chest, Jeni displayed the food. "See? You don't have to worry. We have plenty to eat."

"Oh, boy! Coke!" Tim exclaimed.

"Not now," Jeni said. "You can have one later."

"I want one now," the boy wailed.

Jeni's patience was wearing thin and she silently lectured herself on keeping her cool. "I said, no."

"Okay," he spat, turning on his heel and starting off across the camp, "but you'll be sorry."

"Timmy! You come back here."

The angry youngster kept going.

Jeni quickly caught up with him, grasping his arm. "Timmy," she said as calmly as she could, "you're to *stay with me*."

"No. I won't," he hissed. "Alex was all wrong about you. I shouldn't have listened to him. I hate you!" Letting loose a string of expletives that would have made a longshoreman blush, he wrenched his arm free and started to run.

Brad stepped out from behind his truck to block Tim's way, and hoisted him off the ground by his armpits. "Hey," he said with a low, menacing growl, "where do you think you're going?"

The boy was obviously still angry, but also frightened. He faced Brad squarely, his dark eyes wide and sparkling. "Let—let me go," he demanded.

Jeni jogged up to them. "I'll take him."

"Will you?" Brad drawled cynically. "And what makes you think this miniature Al Capone will stay?"

Biting her lower lip, Jeni was embarrassed to find her eyes filling with tears. Tim had said he hated her, and now Brad was ganging up on her, too. She mustn't cry, she told herself. She mustn't show weakness. *And*, she mustn't let Brad hurt Tim.

Brad saw the misery in her face. Looking Tim straight in the eye, large dark eyes pitted against small dark eyes, he spoke the harsh truth. "Look, kid," he said, nodding toward Jeni, "you're not going to hurt your mother like that again. Do I make myself clear?"

"She—she's not my mother," Tim stammered.

"Brad, stop it," Jeni cut in, reaching to grab his arm.

"And you keep out of this," Brad hissed at her, returning his attention to the small burden he still held off the ground. "That lady has given up everything for you, you little punk, and she's the closest thing you've got to a mother. If I were you, I'd smarten up and start treating her with the respect she deserves, or you'll have to deal with me, too. Got that?"

Timmy swallowed hard. "Y-yes, sir."

"And no more stunts like the one you just pulled?"

"No, sir."

Jeni couldn't believe her ears. "Brad," she ordered, "that's enough."

"Not quite," he said firmly. Putting Tim down, he crouched on the ground next to him, speaking quietly and calmly. "Look, son, I know it's a freaky trip being stuck out here in the middle of nowhere, but believe me, you'll get to like it." He gave the boy a wide grin and put his arm around him. "You've got to remember that adults get scared too, sometimes." Brad whispered in Tim's ear, "I'll bet Jeni's just as uptight as you are right now."

Timmy's eyebrows raised and he glanced quickly at her. "You—you think so?" he asked Brad.

"Yeah, I think so," Brad said softly. "Promise me you'll give her a fair chance to learn all this mother stuff?"

Nodding, Tim started to extend his hand, changed his mind, and wrapped both thin arms around Brad's neck. "Thanks, mister," he whispered before he let go.

Brad got to his feet, clearing his throat noisily. "You're quite welcome, Tim," he said, offering the handshake the boy had instigated earlier.

Shaking hands, Tim turned to Jeni. "I'm sorry."

"That's all right, Timmy," she said flatly. "You go back to camp. I'll be there in a minute."

Obediently, the boy did as he was told.

"*I* could have handled it," she told Brad angrily. "You had no right to interfere and speak to him that way."

"It worked." He seemed pleased with himself.

"And you felt it necessary to threaten him? That's hardly a loving method of control."

"Isn't it? Seems to me he understood my methods better than yours."

"That's not quite the point, is it?" she fumed. "He's *my* son and I'll take care of his discipline. Understand?"

"Perfectly." Brad flashed her a disarming grin. "You don't have to thank me now. I can wait."

Thoughts of hell freezing over popped into Jeni's mind, but she squelched the desire to express them. "Just leave my son alone," she said.

Nodding in acquiescence, Brad pointed to Jeni's camp, indicating a problem.

"Timmy!" she called, seeing him rummaging through her ice chest.

The boy looked at her and stiffened, a cold can of soda in his hand. Brad stood behind Jeni, his arms folded across his chest. As Tim's gaze reached him, Brad slowly shook his head no. Tim smiled sheepishly and dropped the can back into the cooler, closing the lid.

"You see?" she insisted, whirling to face Brad. "There's really no problem."

His eyebrows raised. "So, I see."

Well, she thought, that was better. Jeni softened slightly. "I don't mean to be ungrateful, it's just that Tim and I need time to get to know each other without outside interference. You do understand?"

"Sure," Brad said agreeably, "but remember where the boy comes from, O'Brien. He's used to playing by different rules than you are."

"And you remember," she bristled, "that I'm a trained professional. There's very little you can tell me that I don't already know." Turning, she strode stiffly back to her camp.

Watching her go, Brad resigned himself to her wishes. That boy was more of a handful than she suspected, he thought, but he *was* Jeni's. If she didn't want help, so be it. Brad cringed, imagining what might happen if she didn't take her blinders off and see Tim for what he was—a scared kid with built-in defenses a foot thick. She loved the boy, Brad acknowledged with a touch of internal anguish, but that love could be her undoing—and Tim's—if she didn't start turning it into a tough love.

Ironic, he thought, that love could be a negative force as well as positive. What's this, Carey, getting philosophical? he taunted himself. What else about love have you finally figured out, huh?

He'd planned to move on once he'd seen that Jeni and Timmy were happy. What was stopping him? His glance darted to Jeni's camp. Tim was smugly sipping a can of cola. Damn! That kid had her eating out of his hand. For a smart, strong-willed lady, she sure had an Achilles heel where Tim was concerned. Brad chuckled wryly. It was almost as bad as his own weaknesses where Jeni was concerned, wasn't it?

With a sense of subconscious relief, Jeni watched Brad unload his gear. He was staying. Starting to remember their time together, she forced her attention back to Timmy.

"Come on, sport," she said lightly. "I'll show you some marmots."

Finishing his drink, Tim tossed the can to the ground.

Jeni started to reprimand him, then changed her mind and picked up the can herself. There'd be plenty of time for teaching him manners. For now, she'd simply work on gaining his trust. There was no use alienating him. Taking his hand, she led him onto the campground road.

Carefully skirting Brad's camp, Jeni kept her eyes focused ahead rather than be caught looking his way. Consequently, she didn't see Tim give Brad his most adoring smile and wave covertly at the man he'd already come to admire. Nor, did she see Brad's returning wink and thumbs-up signal.

Sensing a new rapport with the boy, she started to share her feelings. "I'm sorry that man talked to you that way, Tim," she said. "He had no right."

Timmy squeezed her hand, giving a little energetic skip. "It's okay," he said innocently, his eyes aglow with respect for Brad. "You shouldn't be mad at him. He's cool."

Jeni's first reaction was incredulous surprise, then she chuckled. "Well, Tim," she said wryly, "that's one way to put it."

He seemed pleased that she agreed. "Yeah," he said. Smiling up at her, he added, "So're you."

Chapter Seven

Fortunately for Jeni, the marmot colony cooperated by sunning themselves and running over the bare hill that housed their burrows. The fact that Tim compared them to big rats didn't totally thrill her, but at least she'd found something that interested him.

They stopped by the visitors' center before returning to camp and Jeni bought Tim some children's books about nature and a poster of a mountain lion he admired.

Busy getting dinner, she figured he must have been gone at least ten minutes by the time she missed him. Frantic, she called to him.

Tim got to his feet, answering her. "Over here."

Jeni's fears gave way to anger. "What are you doing over there?" she demanded, stalking toward Brad's campsite. "You scared the daylights out of me."

The boy was penitent, but excited. "It's okay," he told her when she'd joined them, "Brad was just showing me how to build a campfire. See?" A small fire blazed brightly in Brad's fire ring.

"I see," Jeni said, gritting her teeth. "He's quite an accomplished outdoorsman."

Timmy missed her sarcasm, but Brad started to laugh quietly.

"Yeah," Tim said enthusiastically, "and he's promised to teach me to fish, too."

Brad was nearly beside himself with repressed mirth.

"Oh, he has, has he?" Jeni said crisply. "I'll bet he can show you how to drive a motor boat, too."

"Wow!" Tim exclaimed, turning to Brad. "Can you?"

A broad smile had spread across Brad's face. "If your mother gives her permission, I guess it would be okay."

Jeni was furious, but not unaware of the latent humor in the whole situation. "I'd planned to teach you all those things myself, Timmy," she told him.

"Oh." The boy went from gleeful to downcast in seconds.

Tim seemed to need a strong male image to follow, she realized. After all, she thought, he had Alex, his older brother, so it really wasn't surprising that Tim felt more comfortable with a man. Jeni considered carefully before offering a suggestion. "I suppose we could *both* take you," she said. "That is, if Mr. Carey doesn't mind."

Brad was quick to agree. "No, Mr. Carey doesn't mind. But I would like you both to call me Brad." He extended his hand to Jeni. "Will you do that, Mrs. O'Brien?"

She was grateful beyond words for his pretense. Taking his hand, she lifted her misty gaze to his in silent thanks. "I'd be delighted—Brad."

Timmy was tugging at the lower edge of her jacket. He whispered when she bent down, "Let's ask Brad to dinner."

There was no suppressing the giggle Jeni felt erupting. "You think we should, huh?"

Tim nodded rapidly.

She stood. "My son wants me to ask you to join us for dinner," she said. "It seems your charms are never-ending."

Brad bowed. "One can only hope. I'd be delighted. What time?"

Grabbing his hand, Tim shouted, "Now!" and began to drag him toward their campsite, leaving Brad to shrug helplessly at Jeni and give her a sheepish smile.

With soft laughter and a shake of her head, Jeni gave up and followed them.

"All right, you guys," she said, "you're here, so you can work for your supper. I'll need more wood before I'm done."

Tim looked beseechingly at Brad. "We men don't have to do stuff like that, do we?" he asked seriously.

Getting to his feet, Brad reached for the boy. "Surprise, Tim. Dinner around here is a community project. Come on. I'll show you the kind of sticks to gather."

She started to call after them to be careful and stay together, but stopped herself. Tim was safe with Brad, she knew. Safer than she was, Jeni thought cynically. What a strange situation they were all in. She and Brad were acting like strangers. Only Tim seemed at home in the company of them both, and *he* was the newcomer. Jeni rolled her eyes skyward. Would wonders never cease!

Laughing and joking around the campfire after dinner, Brad and Jeni both showed Timmy how to roast marshmallows. When his head began to nod, Brad carried the boy to the tent, slipped off his shoes and jacket, and zipped him into his sleeping bag.

"You promise we'll go fishing, tomorrow?" Tim asked sleepily.

"I promise, son," Brad said quietly. Straightening, he returned to the fire and Jeni. "Well, I guess I'd better say good night."

"I guess so." Her eyes were fixed on the flames.

Brad squatted beside her. "I want you to know I didn't put him up to it," he explained. "Timmy came over and started asking questions, and the old teacher in me came out, I suppose. It just seemed natural to show him things."

"I know."

"He's very quick to learn," Brad told her, sure she'd be glad to hear it.

Jeni shook her head. "Unfortunately, that's not what the schools have said."

"Schools? Plural?"

She nodded. "He must have been in at least eight by now. Every time he ran away he'd be placed in another foster home in a new area and presto—a new school. He barely got settled anywhere, but they all agreed he was slow."

"You're kidding." That didn't fit with Brad's own observations of Tim's abilities.

"Nope. Truancy was the reason he was placed in detention in the first place. If I can keep him in school, it'll be a minor miracle." She fell silent staring at the fire.

Brad got to his feet. "Well, I guess I'd better turn in. I've promised Tim we'd fish tomorrow." He paused. "You—you will go with us, won't you?" he asked haltingly.

"You bet," she replied, standing. "I'll have to buy another day's time on my out-of-state license, but it'll be worth it to see *you* teach someone to fish."

"I had a great teacher, myself," Brad teased. "Maybe you've heard of her—Lois Lane?"

Jeni blushed. "Shhh!"

Extending his hand, Brad waited for her to take it, then brought her fingers to his lips. He'd intended to say good night and make some more light banter, but the feel of her hand, the slightly smoky odor of her warm flesh, undid him. Brushing a soft, wordless kiss across her trembling hand, he released her, turned quickly, and left.

Jeni recalled the first night he'd walked away like that after the marshmallow incident. The similarities were striking. Except then, she remembered, they hadn't known anything about each other, hadn't shared intimacies that made the parting even more poignant.

Her hand still tingled from the touch of his lips, and she clasped it tightly in her other hand, sinking to her knees by the fire. She was suddenly very, very cold.

Mrs. Andrews did a double take as Jeni, Brad, and Timmy came through the lodge door.

"Well, well," she quipped, "*that* was fast."

Jeni blushed, Brad laughed, and Timmy looked at all the adults as if they were crazy.

"What can I do for you folks today?" the older woman asked, her eyes twinkling. "A boat and marshmallows?"

"I'd like you to meet Tim, Mrs. O'Brien's son," Brad said. "He'd like to learn how to fish."

Mrs. Andrews offered her hand and Tim took it. "Pleased to meet you, Tim," she said. "Did you just get to Utah?"

"Uh-huh," Tim said. "I'm almost adopted."

"Almost, huh?" Mrs. Andrews echoed. "I think that's wonderful."

"It's okay, I guess." Tim walked away from her, found the shelves piled high with cookies and other treats, and stood dreamily contemplating the available goodies.

"How long have you had him, dear?" Mrs. Andrews asked Jeni.

"I just got custody." Jeni was hurt that Tim hadn't expressed it more enthusiastically, and the older woman seemed to understand.

"These things take time," she said. "Give the boy a chance to get used to the changes."

Jeni shrugged. "I know."

Mrs. Andrews glanced at Brad. "You know, he looks a lot like your friend, here."

Chuckling, Brad agreed. "He kind of does, doesn't he?"

"Not at all!" Jeni exclaimed. "Why, Timmy's a lot——"

"Shorter," Brad said. "Otherwise, we're the same— dark, handsome, charming, witty, lovable . . ."

"And modest," Jeni added.

"I'd like some cookies," Timmy chimed in. "I like these, and these, and . . ."

"Ah, and I forgot about being easy to please," Jeni said.

Joining Tim at the cookie rack, Brad told him to choose one package.

Tim started to complain, but subsided when he noticed the firm expression on Brad's face. He handed Mrs. Andrews a package of chocolate chip cookies, then stuffed his hands resolutely in his jacket pockets.

Brad was preparing to pay for the boat when Jeni objected.

"Nonsense," he insisted. "This is my trip and I'll pay for it." He turned to Mrs. Andrews. "I'd also like to rent a life jacket for the boy. Those float cushions are okay for adults, but I want a permanent vest for Tim."

Objecting vociferously, Timmy shied away from the bulky yellow jacket. "I won't wear that funny-looking thing. I won't!"

Brad only shrugged. "Okay. But no jacket, no boat, and no fishing on the lake. If you fall in, I'm not about to dive in to save your stubborn little neck."

"Brad!" Jeni couldn't believe he'd talk that way to Tim. "Couldn't we carry the life jacket?" She put a hand reassuringly on Tim's shoulder.

"Are you going to guarantee he won't get excited and fall overboard?" Brad asked flatly. "Well, can you?"

"Of course not, but he can wait to put it on until we get into the boat."

"Will you wear it then, Tim?" Brad asked.

Nodding in acquiescence, Tim begrudgingly took the life jacket.

"Good. You carry it." Brad handed the cookies and extra fishing tackle he'd bought to Jeni. "You two can start unloading the truck. I'll settle up and be out in a minute. Tim, you open the door for her," he instructed, watching to make sure the boy did it.

The twinkle in Brad's eye as he watched Jeni and Tim was unmistakable. They were an unlikely pair, but he could see definite possibilities. Tim just needed to learn a new set of rules to function in the society where he was now. And how much could *he* help in the seven days she had left? Brad wondered. Would Jeni have seen, by the time her vacation was over, what it was the boy really needed?

He paid Mrs. Andrews and was about to leave when Jeni came back in, an embarrassed look on her face.

"What is it?" Brad asked.

She wasn't about to tell him. "Go on. I'll be there in a second."

Curious, Brad joined Timmy outside. The boy was eating a candy bar. "Where's Jeni going?" Brad asked him.

"She's dumb," Tim observed, munching happily.

"Oh? Why?"

Timmy held up the candy. "I got away with it and she's going to pay for it. That's dumb, huh?"

"You're absolutely right," Brad said, grabbing the surprised boy by his jacket collar. "*You're* the one who needs to apologize and pay for the candy."

"Hey! Put me down." Kicking and struggling, Timmy

was dragged through the door, the damning candy still clutched in his fist.

Brad slapped his hand over the dollar Jeni had laid on the counter while she was making an explanation to Mrs. Andrews.

"I can take care of it, Brad," she said vehemently.

"Did you steal it?" Brad asked her.

"Of course not!"

"Well, then, I think our sticky-fingered little friend here has something to say to Mrs. Andrews." Lifting Tim to his own eye-level, he stared him down. "Well?"

Tim shook his head violently, averting his eyes from the angry man.

Brad put him down, but didn't let go. "Look, kid," he hissed, crouching by the boy, "what you did before was your business, but when you pull a stunt like this now, it reflects on your mother, too. You understand?"

No answer.

He gave the boy's shoulders a gentle shake. "I said, you got that?"

Tim nodded, his eyes downcast, and tried his best to swallow the candy that seemed stuck in his throat.

"You think that's fair? You think you should let her take the fall for you?"

With a barely discernible shake of his head, Tim said, "No."

"Then what are you going to do about it?"

The boy looked beseechingly at the lodge owner. "I—I'm sorry."

But Brad wasn't through. "Okay. That's a good start. Now, pay for it."

Wide-eyed, Tim stared at Brad. "I don't have any money!"

Reaching into his pocket, Brad produced the proper change. "As of now," he said, handing the coins to Tim, "you own me this much. And I'll expect you to pay it back or work it off. You got that?"

Tim lovingly fingered the coins, then slowly laid them on the counter. "Yes, sir."

When they were outside, Jeni gave vent to her feelings. "You didn't have to embarrass him like that, did you?"

"Would you rather be embarrassed yourself, Jeni?" he asked with careful control of his voice.

The unmistakable gentleness she heard was such a contrast from the scene in the lodge, she hesitated. Had it all been an act for Tim's benefit? Was the roughness and anger only a ploy? Well, it didn't matter. Brad had still been out of line. "*I* will handle his discipline from now on." She parroted his instructions to Tim, "Have *you* got that?"

Raising his hands in mock surrender, Brad asked, "Truce?" A small smile crept across his face as he looked at her. It wouldn't do to be quarreling all day and be stuck in the same small boat, he realized.

So did she. "Okay," she said, leading the way to the dock. "Let's go fishing."

Jeni let Brad pilot the boat, holding her breath for fear he'd botch the job and disillusion Timmy. But all went well and they were soon anchored in the shallow cove across from the cut.

With no further argument, Tim had donned the life jacket, and she found herself grateful that Brad had insisted, feeling more relaxed about her son's excited movements in the boat. Rigging her own pole, Jeni left Brad to prepare Tim's, laughing inwardly at the laborious pains he took with the fishing gear. Her line was in the water by the time Brad got the swivel and leader fastened on Tim's line.

"Look in that bag of stuff we just bought and give me a number twelve hook," Brad told Tim.

Pawing futilely through the packages, Timmy told him there weren't any twelves.

"Sure there are. I bought sixes, eights, and twelves."

Tim was adamant. "Uh-uh. She must've sold you the wrong ones." He held up the plastic packages of hooks. "You got sixes, eights, and twenty-ones."

Brad's brow furrowed, a thoughtful look on his face. Maybe Tim's dislike of school had a basis in a learning problem. The idea was worth pursuing, he decided quickly. "Give me the twenty-ones." He took the hooks from Tim. The package was clearly labeled twelve. "Come over here a minute." Holding up a blue and white cardboard that said, "fish hooks" on the bottom, Brad pointed to the word *fish*. "What does this say, Tim?"

Flustered, the boy looked away. "Who cares? Are we gonna fish, or not?"

Taking a deep breath, Brad put the cardboard back in the bag. That *was* it, Brad thought, not really surprised. Tim's inability to read explained a lot of things. "We're going to fish," Brad said lightly. "We can't let your mom get the best of us, can we?"

Tim seemed relieved. "Nope. We're gonna beat the pants off her, huh?"

Brad nearly choked on a strangled laugh while Jeni turned a bright shade of crimson.

"Something like that," Brad replied, giving her a mischievous wink as his mind proceeded to diagnose Tim's problem. No wonder he'd repeatedly run away, Brad thought. It was obvious he couldn't decipher even simple words and statistically, truants had a high incidence of learning disabilities. Why hadn't the boy been spotted as a probable case of dyslexia? he reflected. Where were the teachers who were supposed to see these things? Brad found himself getting angry. How could they have missed it?

He put his arm protectively around Timmy's shoulders. It must be hell to find yourself an outcast everywhere you've been; first at home, then at school, too. School should have been the one place he could get help, the one place where he'd be understood and cared for. And they'd blown it.

How many schools had Tim been in? he wondered. Perhaps that was the real problem. Passed from district to district, running away to avoid facing his lack of reading ability, Tim had probably never stayed in one place long enough to be given special help.

"Tell me about your brother," Brad urged, wanting to know more about Tim's earlier life.

"Nothin' to tell," Timmy said. "Alex got caught, that's all."

"You miss him?" Brad asked, pretending to watch his fishing pole and line.

Tim swallowed hard, then lied convincingly, "Nope."

"Is he going to get to see him once in a while?" Brad asked Jeni.

"I'll do what I can," she said seriously. "Alex is good for Tim. He tells him not to make the same mistakes *he* did."

"Sounds like a smart boy," Brad said.

"He's a lot smarter than me," Tim told him. "Alex is *real* smart."

Brad touched Tim's hair. "There's nothing wrong with you, either, Tim, that the right teacher couldn't help you fix."

"I hate teachers!"

Jeni laughed. "You sure?"

"I'm sure. Teachers are gross, and mean, and ugly, and—and *dumb*."

Brad laughed as well. "Some are, that's for sure, but you shouldn't condemn them all. That would be like my saying all little boys are stinkers. Is that fair?"

Tim was thoughtful. "I guess not. How come you like teachers so much?"

Jeni was laughing aloud. Let's see Brad get himself out of this one, she mused.

"Well, I hate to tell you this, Tim," Brad said with a deadpan expression, "but I was once one of those teachers you said you didn't like."

"Naw! You couldn't be. You're—you're cool."

"Sorry," Brad shrugged, "but I really was a teacher."

"Ick," Tim said, looking at the big man with an almost visible distaste. After pondering his new idol, though, Tim seemed to come to terms with his own prejudices. "I—I guess you'd be an okay teacher," he said slowly, " 'cause you're okay the rest of the time."

Ah, Brad thought, good. If Tim accepts me as a teacher, maybe that respect will carry over into his future schooling. I can only hope, and once I tell Jeni what I suspect, she can go ahead and pursue the best course of action. It'll probably mean a special class for Tim, for a while at least, but I think it's been caught soon enough.

Jeni bested them both by catching the first trout. It was a beauty and Timmy jumped and hollered so much she finally had to tell him he'd scare away all the other fish if he didn't quiet down.

"She's good, huh?" he said proudly to Brad.

"She's the best," Brad agreed, his eyes bathing her in a glow of remembered ecstasy. He decided it was time to share some of the glory he'd received from Tim. "She's the one who taught me to fish," Brad confessed.

Jeni felt warm and cherished. He hadn't needed to tell Tim, to try to elevate her in the boy's eyes. She honestly hadn't minded Tim's temporary hero-worship of Brad, and it had given her an excuse for the three of them to do something together.

Looking at Jeni, Tim obviously doubted Brad's sincerity.

She nodded affirmatively and the boy stared back at Brad. "She really did?" Tim asked. "Honest?"

"Honest, son. Your mom's a super fisherman and camper."

Tim's dark eyes sparkled happily. "All right!" he said to her, reeling in his line. "Will you fix my hook like yours so I can catch a fish, too?"

Smiling broadly, Jeni baited the hook. "There's no guarantee, honey. Sometimes, the fish are just too smart for us."

"Not too smart for you, huh?" he asked, beaming at her adoringly.

Brad settled back against the seat. Well, step one was accomplished, he thought with satisfaction. Some of the respect had been transferred successfully. Now, all he had to do was get Jeni to see that Tim needed a firm hand, tell her of the dyslexia he suspected, and he could walk away and not worry about them. A sudden twinge of loneliness surprised him, but he shrugged it off. Sure, he'd miss them. They'd both gotten under his skin. Still, that was no reason to feel uneasy. They'd make out fine without him. After all, he had no home, no profession, no roots. No woman would consider . . . No. That was ridiculous. Besides, Jeni had said their relationship was over. It was only because of Tim that she'd accepted his company today. He felt her gaze upon him.

Catching Brad's eye, Jeni mouthed a silent, "Thank you," before turning back to her son. She supposed Brad had done it to relieve himself of the boy's constant attention, but it didn't matter why he'd spoken on her behalf. The important thing was that he had.

He was a wise, kind man, Jeni decided, to try to pass his closeness with Tim along to her. In seven days she and Tim would leave the mountains—and Brad. When

that time came, she could now see, Brad would have prepared Timmy well for the parting.

Yes, she thought as a dull ache grew in her chest, but
who will prepare me?

Chapter Eight

❧

As their day on the lake slowly passed, Jeni felt even better about the relationship between Brad and Tim. It seemed to be a working friendship and Brad certainly needed to make a lot of changes in his attitudes where children were concerned. Perhaps knowing Tim would help him make those changes, she thought, or at least mellow him to the point where he might someday make a decent father. Jeni was seized by deep sorrow almost instantly, fighting it with anger. Why should the thought of Brad as a father bother her? she fumed. Even with the progress he'd made with Tim, he still wasn't the kind of parent she'd want for her son. Brad was far too severe. It was ridiculous to equate the man with any of her ideals about the person she might someday choose to share her life. He didn't fit. He didn't!

Being near him too much was messing her up mental equilibrium, she concluded. As the day went on, Jeni formulated a workable plan of defense. It served two purposes, keeping her busy and giving her a concrete set of goals to shoot for. She would explain to Brad that she and Tim needed time alone, then take the boy for hikes and drives that removed them both from Brad's sphere of influence. If that method failed, she'd leave Cedar Breaks and camp elsewhere. That thought tugged at her heart; loving The Breaks as she did, leaving would be a last resort.

Tim caught several fish, exclaiming loudly that they were bigger and better than those either adult had landed as he half carried, half dragged the heavy creel up the dock toward shore. His smile nearly split his face when Ronnie complimented him on the catch.

Brad and Jeni followed Tim up the gently rocking dock. Taking courage from the presence of Tim and Ronnie, Jeni started to speak out regarding her most recent decision. "Brad, I . . ."

He'd been working on the best way to explain his suspicions about Tim, and he began at the same time. "I need . . ."

They both laughed, started again, and spoke simultaneously.

"You first," Brad told her. "I can wait."

"Actually, I was planning on asking you to come over for a talk this evening after Tim goes to bed." The expectant look on Brad's face made her quickly explain further. "What I *mean*, Mr. Carey, is strictly on the up and up. I honestly do want to talk."

Brad made a sad, silly face. "No moonlight tryst?"

Fighting to control her voice while her emotions soared out of sight, Jeni said, "No. No tryst, just a talk."

"And no Lois Lane and Superman, either, I suppose," he added. "Pity." With a deep, audible sigh, Brad left her and joined Tim. If she wanted to talk, he could probably find a suitable way to tell her about the boy's problems. He knew from experience that parents often look the news of a disability as a personal affront, but he felt he could make it clear to Jeni how lucky she was that Tim was only eight years old and could get a good start on overcoming his handicap.

Reaching into his truck, Brad produced his camera. "Want a picture of you and your fish, Tim?" he asked.

Still beaming proudly, the boy nodded.

"Okay. Stand over there and hold up the biggest ones for me." Brad snapped the photo.

"When do I get to see it?" Tim asked him.

"I guess I'll mail it to you when I get it developed." He turned to Jeni. "Don't forget to give me your address so I can send Timmy's picture."

She looked sidelong at Brad. "Cute, Carey. Real cute. Is that how you get addresses and phone numbers from all your acquaintances?"

"No. I save that approach for special occasions." He focused his attention back to the boy. "Tim, I think I've figured out a way for you to pay me back for the candy. But first, we need to return this life vest."

Jeni obligingly took it, glad to escape his teasing, and headed for the lodge on foot.

Tim looked anything but thrilled to be reminded of his earlier transgression. He muttered a low, "Okay."

Leading the way to a raised wooden platform, Brad pointed to the trough and faucets.

"This contraption is for cleaning fish, Tim. Now, it happens that I *hate* to clean fish," Brad said with exaggerated seriousness, "so I've decided that's how you can work for me." He put the first trout on the block of wood in the trough, stood behind Tim, and gave him his knife. "Start here, by cutting the head off."

It was all Brad could do to keep from laughing at the miserable face Tim made, but the boy did as he was told with little help. As they progressed in the cleaning chore, Tim's curiosity got the better of him and Brad found himself explaining what made fish tick. Viewed scientifically, the internal organs lost their distasteful aura and became simply objects worthy of study.

They were on their third fish by the time Jeni returned, stepped up on the platform, and tried to take over. "You don't have to do that kind of job, Timmy," she said, shooting Brad a frigid stare. "I'll do it."

"No!" Tim said excitedly. "This is neat." He proceeded to name the anatomical portions of the fish. "And this one was a female," he told her. "See? There were eggs inside."

Brad had wisely remained silent.

"I see," Jeni said. "How . . . nice."

"Besides," Tim continued, "I'm working."

She raised her eyebrows disdainfully at Brad. "I see."

Patting the boy on the shoulder, Brad told him his debt was paid in full. "At twenty-five cents a fish, I actually owe you money," Brad said.

"You do?" Tim looked up at him, a smile on his face. "How much would you owe me if I cleaned *all* the fish?"

Laughing, Brad told him.

Jeni gingerly inspected the cleaned fish. They were anything but a professional job.

"Really, Tim," she began, "if you want money, all you have to do is ask me."

Brad released his steadying hold on the knife, cupped Jeni's elbow, and took her aside.

"Look," he said, trying to choose his words carefully, "the kid needs to develop a sense of worth, right?"

How could she disagree? "Right, but—"

"But, nothing. If he'd had any money this morning, maybe he wouldn't have taken the candy."

She started to open her mouth in protest, but Brad silenced her with a raised hand.

"I know, I know. Old habits die hard. Chances are, he'd have stolen it anyway. The point is, he won't have to the next time, and maybe, *just maybe*, he'll pay for what he wants."

"But I can give him whatever he needs."

"Yes, you can." He paused. "Is that the way you were raised? Was everything handed to you?"

She shook her head. "There was very little to hand to me. We didn't have much."

"Well, we did," he said in a reminiscent voice. "And I remember being really angry with my father for making me do chores in order to receive my allowance. It was only as an adult that I saw the wisdom of his discipline." Leaning back against the end of the table, Brad gazed thoughtfully at the lake. "If anything is too easy, Jeni, it loses its worth in a person's eyes. But if it's hard fought for and hard won, it takes on a special importance." His deep brown eyes searched hers. "Give Timmy a fight you know he can win—a job you know he can do—and watch him blossom."

She looked back at Tim, his concentration focused on the fish he was trying to clean, his tongue sticking out one side of his mouth in concentration.

"Okay, this time," she consented, sensing the rightness of Brad's move. "He did owe you for the candy. But after today, no more."

Brad nodded. "Good. Now, let's check on his progress. That's a pretty sharp knife and I don't want him to hurt himself."

All evening Jeni rehearsed her speech to Brad. Tim had insisted they share the fish he'd cleaned, so dinner was again a threesome. This had to stop, she told herself, conscious of Brad's continuing presence with an ever-growing intensity. She was to the point, she had to acknowledge, where being around him much more would bring her to an emotional overload. Her hands shook, her heart seemed in a perpetually accelerated state, and her nerves were becoming so frayed she'd felt on the verge of either anger or tears all through dinner. How she'd managed to hide her agitation, she didn't know. That was, of course, assuming she'd hidden it.

Brad had seemed so preoccupied himself, it was impossible to tell.

When Tim confessed he'd never eaten fish before, the meal became a lesson in avoiding bones while enjoying your catch. He didn't seem overly fond of the main course but ate it just the same. Every once in a while, Jeni noticed, he'd slip his hand into his pocket, listen for the jingle of coins, then smile and go on eating.

The rigors of the full day caught up with Timmy before he'd finished his dinner. Yawn after yawn he struggled against encroaching sleep. Finally, the tired little boy gave up.

"I'm sleepy," he said.

Jeni took his plate. "That's okay, honey. You ate most of your fish. Why don't you turn in?"

Joining her, Brad helped clear the table. Being with her and Tim had made him feel even closer to her, rather than the opposite. Funny, he thought, he'd expected the boy to separate them, but his reaction had been one of affection for both Jeni and Tim. Maybe she was feeling it, too. He decided it was worth finding out.

Coming up behind her, Brad gently grasped her upper arms, flattening himself against her, and felt her jump, then stiffen noticeably. He lowered his head, his cheek on her hair, and said, "Jeni?"

Momentarily holding her breath, Jeni closed her eyes. Damn! Why did he have to touch her? Didn't he know he was only making matters worse? Or did he even care? she wondered irrationally. Whatever she'd planned to say to him had better be said firmly—and soon.

Pulling free, she put distance between them, then faced him. "Brad," she said, fighting a tremor in her voice, "I've come to a decision.

"Sounds serious." He leaned back against the table, one foot on the bench, and crossed his arms. "Okay. Shoot."

"Tomorrow, I'm going to take Timmy to Bryce Canyon."

"So?"

"*I'm* taking him—just the two of us."

Brad took a deep breath. "I see. And the next day?"

"The next day, we'll go somewhere else. I haven't picked a trip for each day yet, but I will. I want to show him the country, and I think I should do it alone."

A barely perceptible sag appeared in Brad's shoulders. "Will you be coming back here at night?"

Jeni couldn't look at him anymore. "I suppose. At least for a few more days. I do appreciate your concern for Tim," she said, "it's just that I need him to myself. We hardly know each other."

"I hadn't meant to interfere, you know," he said seriously. "I simply took a shine to the kid. I guess he reminds me a little of myself."

That admission shocked her to the core. "You did? He does? Oh!"

"As a matter of fact, yes," Brad said. This probably wasn't the best time to discuss Tim's problems, but if she was considering leaving the camp he might lose touch with her, and Brad couldn't take that chance. "Remember, I said I'd been a teacher?" he asked unnecessarily, to open the subject.

"Of course. Why?"

"Well, I've had considerable experience with children who have learning disabilities, and I noticed Tim——"

"Wait a minute!" Jeni exploded. "Don't you *dare* tell me you like Tim in one breath and then in the next try to convince me there's something wrong with him."

"Why not? What does one have to do with the other?"

"Everything," she insisted. "You said yourself he's bright. And he learned the parts of a fish in only a few minutes."

"True," Brad said, keeping his voice low and calm, "but he didn't have to read that information, Jeni."

What a hateful way to attack Tim, she thought. Brad had obviously just pretended to like the boy all along. She covered her ears. "You can stop this preposterous fairy tale." she told him. "I don't believe a word you're saying."

Brad approached her, grasped her wrists, and held her fast. "I don't care what you think of me," he lied convincingly, "but you're going to listen to what I think is wrong with Tim because his whole future may depend upon your following through with the proper remedial training."

"You're crazy," she spat. "Let go of me."

His grip tightened. "No. You can be stubborn all you want on your own behalf, but I'll be damned if I'm going to let you ruin that kid's chances."

"Me? Ruin his chances for what?" she screeched.

Brad eyed Tim's tent. "We're too close to him. I need to talk to you privately, especially if you're going to resort to yelling. Come on." Keeping hold of one wrist, he dragged her away from the fire, then through the trees and out into the moonlit meadow.

With her heart thudding, Jeni doubted his assertion that he wanted to talk to her until Brad released her and began to earnestly state his case.

"Think back, Jeni. You were Alex's parole officer. When did Tim start running away?"

She fought to catch her breath. "I—I don't know. A little over two years ago, I guess."

"He was six years old?"

"Yes. Why?"

"That's when most schools start to teach reading."

"What does that——"

"Shh. Let me talk, please." Brad waited till he wa

sure of her attention. "Do you happen to know what percentage of juvenile delinquents have reading problems?"

Jeni just stared at his shadowed face.

"Well, I'll tell you. It's about seventy-five percent, and that's probably a conservative estimate. It's like asking what came first, the chicken or the egg, until you probe into the individual cases. When a kid is placed in a no-win situation, he'll only stay till the pressure becomes unbearable, then he'll run, either by actually leaving, by being socially maladjusted, or by just dropping out mentally. Tim had other problems at home and took off with Alex. Am I right?"

"So far."

"Remember the fish hooks and the numbers?" Brad asked. "He transposed them."

"So? Lots of people do that. I've done it myself."

"True. But you *knew* you did it. He doesn't. He actually sees things backwards. If I'm right about his problem, he needs some special help and he needs it now, before he's much older."

Her breathing was returning to normal, but Jeni was far from ready to accept Brad's opinion. "You seem awfully concerned for a man who hates children," she taunted. "Come on. Admit you're only guessing."

Brad chose to overlook the personal slur. Maybe he did deserve her rancor, but that didn't change his knowledge about Tim. "No. It's more than that, Jeni. Look. Tim picked up the fish anatomy faster than most kids his age would have. He has definite auditory strengths to compensate for visual weaknesses. I can tell you what tests to request when he gets back in school. They'll pinpoint the problem and Tim will be given the help he needs. You won't have to take my word for it." Pausing, he regarded her seriously. "*Please?*"

"You're sure?" He seemed almost desperate to convince her. Perhaps there was some validity to what he was saying.

"Nearly one hundred percent sure," Brad said. "Jeni, honey, no matter what you think of me, don't jeopardize Tim's chances because of it."

Silently, she considered what Brad had told her. "Does this problem you think Tim suffers from have a name?"

"There's a broad term, dyslexia, that covers his difficulty and lots of other reading disabilities. That's as good a name as any, if you have to have a label for it."

Her thoughts flew to Alex. He'd been a runaway for as long as she'd known him. "Could his brother have it too?"

Brad was noncommittal. "It's hard to say."

"I see." Jeni remembered the books she'd bought for Tim and how little interest he'd shown in them. "Maybe all Timmy needs is some private coaching. I got him some books and I can sit down with him and work a little on them every day."

"No, don't," Brad cautioned.

"Why not? Do you want him to learn, or not?"

"Of course I do," he said, "but you need to be careful you don't ask for more than he can give, to begin with. Once you turn him off, it'll be hell getting him to try again."

"Me? Ask for too much? It seems to me you're the one who keeps doing that."

"You mean discipline. That's different. He can handle that because he already understands it. With reading he'll have to have a base to work from before he can go on to actually do it."

So, Brad didn't want her to work with Tim, she saw clearly. Probably because he was trying to make something out of Tim's slowness that would make him indispensible as a tutor. "I'm sorry, Brad," Jeni said flatly. "You almost had me convinced." She turned to go. "Good night."

"No!" Grabbing her arm, Brad held her while she tried to wrench free. "You can't discount what I've said."

"I can, and I do," she hissed. "Timmy's had a whole slew of teachers and not one of them has suggested anything like what you've tried to tell me. Surely, one would have."

"Not necessarily," he said through clenched teeth. "The kid kept taking off—you said so yourself—then winding up in a new school. If a teacher had a big class, he or she might not have gotten Tim tested before he'd gone on to the next school, the next teacher."

The validity of what he was saying almost penetrated Jeni's firmly entrenched prejudices, but not quite. "No," she insisted. "I told you. There's nothing wrong with Tim that a loving home and a stable environment won't cure."

"Lady, you're wrong," Brad said slowly, "about a lot of things."

Suddenly, Jeni sensed Brad was no longer referring to Tim. Her face tilted up to his as if an outside force were compelling it. Her fury melded with latent desire and the difference in the two emotions was hardly discernible.

Brad hadn't intended to kiss her when he'd led her into the meadow. Now, it seemed the *only* thing to do, under the circumstances. He lowered his mouth to hers.

Something in the back of Jeni's mind told her to resist him and she did, but her feeble efforts soon ceased. Relaxing in the familiar circle of his embrace, she melted against him like butter on a hot griddle.

"Ahh," she whimpered, unable to squelch the relief she felt in his arms. Hungrily her mouth moved over his, coaxing and teasing erotically while her hands slipped around his waist.

"Oh, Jeni," Brad said breathlessly, "can't we——?"

"Shh," she pleaded, her lips parting and her tongue brazenly probing his kiss.

Brad's arms tightened around her. God, he'd missed this. There was no disputing it. He'd been with Jeni as a friend, yet missed her as a woman. Memories of their private times together came flooding back to him and he slid a hand under her sweater. He was driven. He *had* to touch her. Surely, she couldn't be angry enough to deny him—not considering the way she was responding.

Unfastening the buttons on his shirt, Jeni slipped her hands inside, reveling in the warm, familiar feel of his chest. She teasingly played her fingers through the fine, dark hairs, murmuring a caress against his lips. Her whole body had been aflame the moment he'd kissed her, and she was secretly glad Brad had defied her decision to remain apart.

He drew his hand softly across her cheek. "Jeni, we can't stay here in the open, so close to camp."

Brad was right, she knew. Still, if they moved would it break the mood? And where could they go? She couldn't just walk off with Timmy asleep in the tent. After all, he was only eight.

They walked arm in arm back to her camp. "Come with me," Brad urged tenderly.

Jeni eyed her tent. "But, Timmy . . ."

"He'll be okay. He'll never know you're gone."

That was probably the truth. "I should look in on him, Brad. He went to bed by himself, and I . . ."

"We'll both check on him," Brad said.

Jeni tried to lift the tent flap without disturbing her son. Tim looked so lost, swallowed up in the full-sized sleeping bag. His head turned to her, his dark eyes misty from slumber. Gently, she smoothed a lock of hair off his forehead.

Looking up at her, Tim said, "I missed you. Where were you, Mommy?"

Jeni's vision clouded and she looked beseechingly up at her lover, then down at her son. Mommy. Tim had called her Mommy for the first time. How could she leave him now?

Brad lifted her to her feet, his gaze filled with the realization he'd lost.

"Brad, I . . ."

"I know, honey," he said. "You have to stay."

She nodded. "I'm sorry."

He tried to sound understanding. "It's okay." Releasing her arm, he stepped back. "And you're going to be gone, tomorrow?"

"Yes."

"But you will come back, won't you?" He couldn't let her just disappear. Whatever the future held, Brad wasn't ready to meet it yet.

"We'll be back." Jeni swallowed hard. "Brad, I—I *do* want to be with you. You know that, don't you?"

"Then come with me." He held out his hand.

She looked at the sleeping boy and shook her head. "If he woke again and I wasn't here, he'd be frightened. He needs me, Brad."

When he replied, his voice sounded detached and nearly expressionless. "And what about you? What do you want?"

"That doesn't matter, does it?" Jeni asked flatly. "I've taken on the responsibilities of a child. He's mine to care for, no matter what. It's not a matter of choice, anymore. The decision was made when I filed to adopt."

"Oh, I get it," Brad retorted sharply, feeling hurt and rejected. "You took him for better or for worse, for richer or for poorer, in sickness and in health, till——"

"Brad, stop it!" Jeni whispered harshly. How dare he ridicule those words. "You're not being fair."

She was right, he thought morosely. He wasn't being

fair, or sensible, or understanding. Brad stuffed his hands in his pockets.

"You're right, O'Brien," he said penitently, "I wasn't."

Jeni had been ready for a fight, and his agreement undid all her preset defenses. "Oh."

Brad went on. "I'm sorry. I—well, I guess I forgot who we both were for a second. It's funny, but when I'm with you it all seems so right and natural that I have trouble remembering we've only recently met and have such different lives." His sense of propriety and fear of further rejection kept him from revealing his true feelings to her. While his heart screamed, "I love you," his lips made no move to repeat the damning confession.

"I can understand that," Jeni said, "because I do it, too."

"You do?" His breathing deepened. Perhaps she'd reconsider, if that was the way she felt. Perhaps they could spend the next few days together, after all. Brad's hopes had just risen when Jeni dashed them to pieces.

"Yes," she declared, "and that's why I want to stay away from you, Brad."

"That doesn't make any sense!"

"Don't you see? It's the only thing that *does* make sense. We don't belong together, as much as our bodies have tried to convince us otherwise. Not only are our backgrounds totally different, so are our probable futures."

"And you can't chance a few days of transitory happiness, Jeni? Why not?"

How could she tell him what was happening to her? This conversation, alone, was tearing her to pieces. It felt like losing James had, except then she'd had no choice. Now, she had to make the decision herself and stick to it no matter what. That was worse—much worse.

Jeni squared her shoulders. "My future happiness is lying asleep in that tent," she said firmly. "I've fought too hard for him to take a chance on wrecking our life by complicating it. I'm sorry, Brad."

He seemed to finally give up the fight. "I see." Turning to go, he glanced back at her. "When you two are here in camp, may I have your permission to visit Tim?"

Her breath caught in her throat.

Seeing her nervous reaction, Brad explained. "I promise I won't bother you, personally. I thought maybe Tim would like to go for an occasional hike or something. That would give you some time to yourself."

When Jeni stared, speechless, he went on, "You've noticed that he needs a man's touch. It might be good for him."

There was no denying Brad's wisdom, she decided. "You're right," Jeni told him. "I guess there'd be no harm in that." She tried to smile. "The way Tim feels about you, I suppose he'd be bugging you, anyway."

"I suppose," he said. "Then it's all right with you?"

"Yes, but . . ." How could she put this without hurting Brad further?

Sensing her dilemma, he said it for her. "I won't allow him to drag us into any more threesomes. Don't worry."

The finality of his tone shook her to the core. Jeni knew if she tried to speak she'd never finish the first few words before breaking down. Tears clouded her vision and sobs choked her throat. Nodding, she turned her back to him, barely able to control herself.

Staring at her, the soft auburn curls, her barely perceptible shudder as she'd turned, the remembered warmth and affection of the open, loving woman that was Jeni, Brad found his eyes filling with a moisture that was foreign to him. After a few moments, he knew he must get away before he disgraced himself.

Never before had he been so moved, cared so much. And never before, he admitted ruefully, had he known the ecstasy and pain of a love like he'd come to feel for Jeni O'Brien.

Chapter Nine

Carefully avoiding Jeni the next morning, Brad saw her drive away with Tim. He'd had to lecture himself sternly to get up at all, and a trip to the lake alone held no appeal. He checked the brochures in the visitors' center and collected them all, formulating a plan as he went along. As soon as Tim came home, he'd begin. The thought of being able to help the boy wasn't enough to dull the aching emptiness in his life that had been filled by Jeni, but anything helped.

It was late afternoon when he saw her car drive through the campground gate. Busying himself gathering firewood, Brad watched her park and slowly get out. She looked tired, he thought. Poor thing. The drive to Bryce was long, according to the maps he'd studied, and Jeni probably hadn't realized what a trying trip she'd let herself in for. He saw Tim jump out, run around the car, and grab Jeni's hand excitedly.

Brad had to look away. They were so touching together, it brought a catch to his throat. He put down the wood and started to clean out his fire ring.

"Hi!" Tim had come up behind him.

Composing his expression, Brad turned to the boy. "Hi, yourself. Did you have a nice trip?"

"Yeah." Tim's hands were fumbling with something under his jacket. He drew out a long, rectangular package. "I brought you a souvenir, since you couldn't come with us." Cocking his head, he exclaimed proudly, "And I *paid* for it, too. No more rip-offs."

Brad gingerly accepted the package. "Thanks, Tim but you shouldn't have spent your money on me."

"That's what she said," Tim told him, gesturing toward Jeni, "but I wanted to."

"And I'm proud you did," Brad added. "Can I open it now?"

"You bet!" Tim said enthusiastically, shuffling his feet with impatience. "Hurry up."

"Okay, okay," Brad said, echoing the boy's excitement. It was a bright orange ruler with tourist-type pictures of fish, trees, and animals.

"I thought you could use it to see how big your fish were, and—and teachers use those all the time, huh?"

"They sure do, pal," Brad agreed. "Thanks." Extending his hand, Brad expected Tim to shake it. Instead, the boy flew into his arms, giving him a fiercely possessive hug.

"Am I really your pal?" Tim asked.

"Sure. Why?" Brad was holding him loosely, looking him straight in the eye.

" 'Cause," Tim said haltingly, " 'cause, I think I got a problem."

Brad tousled the boy's hair. "You want my help?"

With a sincere nod, Tim looked over at Jeni. "It's my, my—it's Jeni," he said. "I think she's sorry she got me."

"That's not true, son," Brad assured him. "I know it's not." He stood and took Tim by the hand. "Let's go for a walk and talk about it, shall we?"

"Could we?" Tim seemed relieved to be able to confide in someone.

"Sure. You go ask your mom if it's okay."

Timmy had dashed to Jeni, obtained her permission, and returned before Brad had finished stacking his firewood. He slipped his hand back into the man's and tugged. "Let's go."

Brad chuckled. "Okay. I'm coming."

They walked away hand in hand, as alike as a natural father and son, and Jeni closed her eyes tight against the sight of the two of them together. Seeing the two people she loved most in the world strike such an intimate pose was more than she could bear. Only the presence of a realistic attitude saved her from fantasizing about the three of them as a real family.

Don't do it, she chided herself caustically. If she did she'd be opening herself to nothing but misery when the bubble burst and she was left with an incomplete picture.

Tim kept glancing back as they entered the broad, gently sloping expanse of the alpine meadow. "You think she can hear?" he asked Brad.

"You mean all the way out here? No. Mothers have great ears, but not that good." Brad seated himself on a red rock ledge, patting the place next to him. "Sit here and tell me what's going on."

The boy's dark eyes pleaded for understanding and loyalty. "You promise you won't tell her?"

"Is it something you've done against the law?" Brad asked gently.

"No! I swear." He raised both palms toward Brad. "I'm clean, honest." He looked suddenly forlorn. "I don't know *what* I did."

Brad placed an arm around Tim's shoulders. "So, tell me what makes you think she's sorry she has you."

Timmy's eyes filled with tears and it was all Brad could do to remain authoritative. "She—she cried last night. Almost all night." A tear slid down Tim's cheek and he wiped it away with the sleeve of his jacket. "I heard her."

"Oh, Tim," Brad groaned, folding him in a tight, supportive embrace, "that wasn't your fault."

Tim's tears came like a torrent of rushing water in one of the nearby mountain streams as he finally gave in to his fears and disappointments. "Y-yes it i-is," he stammered, gulping for air. "It ha-has to be."

Holding Timmy closer, Brad cursed himself for the mess he'd made of the whole affair. He let the boy cry till his sobs began to lessen.

"Listen, Tim," Brad said, his own voice nearly cracking in commiseration, "you trust me, don't you?"

Timmy nodded, wiping his eyes, and looked lovingly up at his friend.

"Then believe me. Jeni wasn't crying because of you."

"Then why?"

"It's an adult problem, Tim, but I *know* it's not your fault, and you have to understand that." Digging in his pocket, Brad produced a handkerchief, lending it to the boy. "Here. Blow."

"I wish I could go with *you*, instead of her," Timmy said. His breathing was slowing. He blew his nose again.

If Jeni suspected how Tim's allegiances were growing away from her, Brad knew she'd be terribly hurt. "You mustn't think that," Brad told him. "Jeni loves you very much."

Tim remained sullenly silent.

Brad tried to cheer him. "We can write to each other after you go home." He'd planned to bring up the subject of Tim's schooling, anyway, and the boy had given him the perfect opportunity to make his point.

Tim looked as if Brad had slapped him. "No, we can't," he said in a near whisper. "I can't write."

"Not yet, maybe, but you'll learn."

"No I won't."

"Oh?" Brad asked. "What makes you so sure?"

Timmy kicked at the dirt at his feet, burying the toe of his left sneaker in the red dust. "I just know, that's all. I'm too dumb."

Putting his arm around Tim's shoulders, Brad started to walk, drawing the boy along. "No, you're not. Remember how you learned the parts of the fish?"

He shrugged. "So?"

"So, you did it really fast for your age. I know. I was a teacher." Brad sensed Tim's eyes searching his face to see if he was telling the truth.

"That wasn't the same," Tim said disconsolately.

"In a way it was." Crouching down, Brad smoothed the dirt with his hand, took a small stick, and made the letter T in the dust. "Listen up."

"Okay," Tim said, joining him, curious.

"Every letter in the alphabet has one or more sounds it stands for. If you can remember those sounds like you did the parts of a fish and then say them together, you can read words."

"Naw."

Brad chuckled, giving Tim a playful poke. "Yeah."

When Tim said, "Okay, prove it," Brad knew he was on his way. He started with the letters in Tim, Brad, and Jeni, the names that meant the most to both of them.

Once Tim had committed a sound to memory, he seldom stumbled over it again, and Brad had to practically drag him back to camp as darkness approached.

"We've got a lantern. We can do more letters later, can't we, Brad?" he begged. "Please?"

Laughing heartily, Brad patted him on the head. "I think we've done enough for today. Maybe tomorrow some time we can practice a few more. Now, go on. Your mother looks like she's waiting for you."

Tim held fast to Brad's hand. "Aren't you coming, too?"

"No, son. I can't tonight," Brad alibied.

"Why not?" Tim's gaze darted from Brad to Jeni, and back. "Is she mad at you?"

"No," Brad said tenderly.

"Are you mad at her?"

"No, Tim. Nobody's mad. We just decided not to spend so much time together, that's all."

Tim cocked his head to one side. "You don't like her much, huh?"

A wry half-smile curled Brad's lips. "Well, that's not quite it."

"You do like her then?"

"Okay, you little stinker. I *do* like her."

"Then why———?"

"Oh no you don't," Brad interrupted forcefully. "That's enough personal questions for one evening. Now, *you go home*."

Timmy backed most of the way to Jeni's camp, nearly falling over the rocks on the way.

"Hi, honey," she said greeting him warmly. "Are you hungry?"

"Uh-huh." Tim clambered up to the table, surveyed the food she'd spread out for dinner, and started trying to pick out familiar single letters on the packages.

Jeni's brow furrowed. Tim was certainly acting strangely. "What's the matter, honey? Is there something wrong with the food?"

"Nope," he said, turning the salt container over in his hands. "I'll be right back." A quick dash to Brad's gave him the sound for S and he happily mouthed the word *salt* over and over.

Observing Tim's lightning-fast trip next door and back, Jeni shook her head. "Did you forget something over there?"

"Nope."

"You gave him his present?"

"Uh-huh." Tim stuffed an enormous potato chip in his mouth.

"Did he like it?" For a kid who usually babbles on and on, she thought, he's certainly close-mouthed tonight.

Tim nodded affirmatively. "He said the same thing you did."

This was getting to be almost a game. "Okay, Tim. I'll bite. What did he say?"

Chewing happily, Tim swallowed another chip. "That I shouldn't spend my money on him." Jeni's mouth fell open. "But I told him I did anyway, 'cause I wanted to."

"Timmy," Jeni asked seriously, hoping she'd misunderstood, "did you tell him *I* said that about him?"

"Uh-huh."

"Oh, Timmy," she groaned. "You didn't."

"It's okay," Tim assured her. "He likes you anyway."

Wiping her hands on a towel, she told the boy to stay there and call her if the hamburgers started to look too done. She set the bowl of chips in front of him. "I'll be right back. Don't eat so many you spoil your supper."

Brad saw her coming. At first, he thought she might be angry, but as she got closer he saw her look of embarrassment. Leaning back against the table, one leg propped on the bench, he said, "Hello."

"I came to apologize—and explain," Jeni said nervously.

"For what? Tim behaved himself beautifully this evening."

"Super," she said cynically. "I understand he told you what I said when he wanted to buy you a souvenir."

So, that was it, Brad mused. He *had* noticed a twinge of hurt feelings when Tim had related the scene to him. "Don't worry about it," Brad told her. "I think I can take it." His attempt at humor failed.

"Oh, Brad. There's nothing to take. He didn't tell you all of it."

"You don't have to explain anything to me," he insisted. "You're his mother, or soon will be, and whatever advice you give him is up to you."

"That's the point," Jeni went on. "I didn't tell him not

to get you anything. I simply told him to save his money and I'd pay for it, but he was adamant. He said to be a real good present, it had to be bought with the same money he'd earned." She paused. "You do see how my comment was meant, don't you?"

"Yes, I do."

"But there's more," Jeni said. "I wanted to tell you because I wanted you to know you were right."

"About what?"

"About Tim and his self-respect. I've never seen anything like that kid in the souvenir shop. He must have kept me there for nearly an hour while he looked for the perfect gift for you and tried to match his spending money against the prices. I'll bet I can tell you the price of every memento sold anywhere in the state of Utah!"

Brad chuckled quietly. "I see. How handy for you."

"Thanks." Smiling, Jeni continued. "I watched him like a hawk and he never made a false move. He really did buy your gift, and it was with his own money."

"I know. He swore to me it wasn't a 'hot' present."

"He did?" Jeni began to giggle. "Terrific!"

Brad's smile was broad and genuine. "I thought so, too." He grew more serious. "He's going to make it, Jeni. I know he is."

She agreed, glad for his confidence in Tim. "I know it, too." Staring at Brad, she felt his support flow between them. "Thank you for saying it, though. Sometimes, as the months went by, I was scared."

He did understand. "That's perfectly natural. It's a new life for you, this instant parent stuff."

Jeni relaxed a little more. "Boy, that's for sure," she confessed, "especially a child as young as Tim. I was used to working with delinquents twice his age." Thinking back, she realized Brad had seen the problem long ago. "I guess I coddled Tim too much at first, didn't I?"

"Maybe a little," he said gently. "But don't worry

about it. As long as you're consistent from now on, he'll come around. You'll see."

"I know." Jeni glanced back at Tim, then called to him. "Hey, sport! You watching those burgers?"

Stuffing a handful of chips into his mouth, Tim hopped down from the bench and went to the fire. Quickly swallowing, he nearly choked trying to call to her, managing to squeak out a strangled, "Help!"

Jeni laughed. "I think I'd better go."

"Sounds like it," Brad said, also smiling. "I think you should hurry, from the looks of your dinner." Smoke was rising from the skillet in an ever-increasing cloud.

She started to leave, then stopped. "Will you be in camp tomorrow?"

"I guess so. Why?"

Suddenly, Jeni's smouth felt dry, her pulse an erratic flutter in her chest. "I—well—I thought Tim and I would stick around Cedar Breaks tomorrow. That was a long, tiring trip today and we both need a day to rest up if we're going to see Zion on our next jaunt."

"And?" After all she'd said about staying apart, she was making very little sense to Brad.

"And I thought maybe you'd like to take Tim for a hike, or something. He'd love it." Damn, Jeni cursed silently, you *know* that's not what you wanted to say; not what you want to do. Why don't you admit you hate being away from him and you'd like to take back all that foolishness about not getting together?

"Your dinner's burning," he observed blandly. What did she want from him, anyway? Wasn't it bad enough seeing her from a distance and knowing she'd never again be his? Did she have to come so close, looking and smelling so damned good, and taunt him like this? Brad had thought, when she'd asked what he was going to do the next day, that she was changing her mind about him, but that was evidently not the case.

Jeni darted a glance at her camp. "I know, I . . ." What was the use? she decided, giving up. She should be thankful Brad had been so kind to Tim, although why, she still couldn't fathom. "I'll see you tomorrow, then," she said quickly, and went to rescue the charred hamburgers.

Hunger was the last thing on Brad's mind. He started to light his fire, then decided against it. If he stayed outside, he'd be unable to avoid seeing and hearing her. The thought of the torture inherent in that was more than he could cope with at the time. Straightening up his gear, he secured his camp and went into the camper, flopping down on the bed fully clothed.

If he were sensible, he would pack up and move on, he reasoned. That would eliminate all the idiotic nonsense about Jeni that kept crowding his mind. Her presence was becoming nearly enough to unhinge him, and the loss of his self-control and well-ordered life was getting harder and harder to take. But thoughts of putting an end to seeing her caused him a distress akin to physical pain.

Damn it, he cursed. The only way he was going to get that woman again was to *marry* her. By the time he'd realized what he'd just told himself, his palms were sweaty, his breathing irregular. Impossible! he retorted. Everything's all wrong. Never before had he found himself so ready to chuck the specific, precisely formulated plans he'd made for his life.

Shaking his head, Brad sat up disgustedly. No way was he going to mess up his chances to finally do what he wanted with his future. He'd put in five miserable years as a teacher to secure his grandfather's inheritance for his sisters and himself. Nothing was going to come along and screw up his opportunity to travel leisurely, see the whole country, then settle where he finally decided to invest some of the money he'd sacrificed so much to obtain. Nothing was; not even a gorgeous, loving, intelligent lady or a kid whose simple presence screamed for his help.

Brad removed his clothing with a jerky, preoccupied vexation. No, he kept telling himself. No way. But his mind wouldn't be distracted. He lay for hours wrestling with himself till the weariness of the fight let him sleep.

Shoving a bit of charred meat into his mouth, Tim looked across the table at Jeni, noticing her meal sitting untouched. "Did I ruin them too bad?" he asked sadly.

She snapped out of the reverie she'd courted ever since she'd left Brad. "What?"

Tim pointed to her plate. "Is it too burned?"

"Oh, no, honey." Jeni obligingly took a bite. "It's fine. I'm just not real hungry."

"Oh." He bit into his hamburger again.

"Tim?" she asked slowly, "would you mind if we kind of hung around here, tomorrow? I know I promised to take you to Zion, but I'm kind of tired, and——"

"Heck no!" he sputtered. "Can I go see Brad?"

"Not now," she said, glancing at his empty, quiet camp. "He's gone to bed, I guess."

"No, no," Tim corrected. "I mean tomorrow. Can I go see him tomorrow?"

"Well, sure. If that's what you want to do."

"All day?"

Jeni felt the sting of Tim's exuberance about being with Brad. At least he could have indicated he'd like to spend *some* time with her. She shrugged off her negative feelings. What difference did it make in the long run? she reasoned. The boy needed male influence to help him make the transition to his new life. In time, he'd begin to find her presence adequate. It would come. All she needed was patience.

"Well, honey, I don't think it's fair to Brad for you to

spend the whole day, but we'll see." She glanced at Tim's plate. "Eat your salad, too. It's good for you."

Tim mouthed a hissing sound, recognizing the S at the beginning of *salad*.

"What?"

"Oh, nothing," he quickly assured her. "I was just thinking." He changed the subject. "Do you like him?"

Jeni knew who Tim meant. Still, she asked, "Who?"

"Brad. He likes you."

Suddenly, Jeni wished Tim were an adult; someone she could safely confide in. She swallowed hard. "You ask too many questions."

"That's what *he* said," Tim volunteered.

Jeni choked on a potato chip. "He did?"

"Uh-huh."

What had Tim asked? she nervously wondered. And how had Brad answered? "Um, what did you ask him, Tim?"

"I don't remember." Tim stuffed the last of his bun in his mouth.

"Well, what did you mean, he likes me?" A light flush colored Jeni's cheeks. Remembering her times with Brad, the color grew to a glowing crimson. "Timmy, tell me," she demanded.

Her tone caused the boy to regard her seriously. "He said you guys weren't mad at each other. Are you?"

She breathed a little easier. "No, Tim, we're not mad."

"And you do like him?"

That was the understatement of the year, Jeni mused. "Yes, Timmy, I like him," she confessed. "Why?"

"Nothin'."

"*Timmy!*" she nearly shouted, her emotions so near the surface she thought she'd explode. "What else?"

By this time, Tim seemed unsure whether he should continue. "Don't get mad," he begged.

Jeni fought to calm down. "I'm not mad, Tim," she said more quietly. "Just tell me what else Brad said."

The boy appeared to concentrate. "Oh, yeah. He said you guys had decided not to do stuff together anymore."

"That's all?"

"Yeah." Tim climbed down from the table and carried his paper plate to the trash, mumbling to himself.

"What?" Jeni asked, wondering if he'd recalled something else Brad had said.

Tim stopped. "You'll get mad," he said.

Going over to him, Jeni gently gripped his shoulder. "No, I won't, honey. Tell me what you said, just now. I promise I won't get mad."

Tim pressed his lips together, a habit Jeni noticed was faintly reminiscent of Brad. "I—I said it was dumb," he whispered, his eyes downcast. "If you like somebody, you shouldn't be that way."

Jeni hugged him close, then looked him in the eyes, cupping his cheeks in her hands. "You're a very smart boy, Tim, do you know that?" She expected him to contradict her the way he had before when she'd mentioned school, but he didn't.

"Yeah," he said happily, a grin covering his face. "I am pretty smart."

Chapter Ten

A stirring in the tent woke Jeni just after dawn.

"Hey, quiet down, Tim," she muttered, reaching out her arm to drape it over him. His sleeping bag was empty. Jeni sat bolt-upright. "Tim?" She rubbed her eyes. "Timmy?"

The tent flap was untied. Poking her head out into the crisp, cold morning air, she saw Tim bounding over the rocks between her camp and Brad's. As early as it was, she knew she'd wake other campers if she shouted to Tim, and she couldn't very well pursue him in her nightgown. "Timmy," she hissed disgustedly to no avail, "Timmy!"

Struggling quickly into her clothes, Jeni crawled out of the tent. She'd pulled on her tennis shoes without tying them and nearly fell when she stepped on a loose shoelace. "Damn!" Jeni crouched, tying her shoes. "That kid," she grumbled, stalking over the rocks.

Tim had long since disappeared into the camper. Pausing with her hand raised to knock, Jeni hesitated, then rapped on the metal door.

"Grand Central Station," Brad's voice announced from inside the camper. "Take a number."

Jeni was embarrassed for having disturbed him further, but she couldn't let Tim run all over him without permission. "Is my son in there?"

"You mean a good-looking kid with messy hair, a big smile, and his shoes on the wrong feet? Yeah," Brad called back. "You want him?"

"I sure do," Jeni said firmly. "He's in big trouble for bothering you."

Pulling on his jeans, Brad ran his fingers along his face and felt the stubble of a beard shadowing his chin. "Just a minute." He opened the door a wide crack. "You lose something, lady?" he asked with a small, rakish smile.

The sight of his bare chest and sleepy-eyed look did strange things to Jeni's equilibrium. She found herself speechless from the intimate memories his appearance triggered.

Brad opened the door farther. "Would *you* like to come in too?"

"Uh—no, thank you," she said breathlessly. "I want to apologize for Tim, though."

Smiling at her, Brad left the door open and sat on the edge of the bed rubbing the sleep from his eyes. "I did say he could come over, didn't I?" Brad conceded. "Next time, I'll have to remember to be more specific about the time."

Tim was bent over, looking at his tennis shoes. "They are *not* on the wrong feet," he protested loudly.

The adults uttered a unanimous, "Shhh!"

Jeni yawned, covering her mouth. "I really am sorry, Brad."

He joined her in a yawn and a languid stretch. "It's okay."

Gesturing boldly to Tim, Jeni said, "Front and center. Now." The boy made a face, then complied. Good, Jeni thought, he may disagree with me, but he's behaving himself. She lifted his downcast face, looking him in the eyes. "Home, young man, and no side trips."

"I—I forgot to go to the bathroom this morning," Tim complained. "Can I go there, first?"

"Okay," she agreed, "but then march straight home."
Her arm was extended stiffly toward her camp. Watching
Tim shuffle off down the path, Jeni was seized with a rush
of love for her son. Deep in thought, she failed to notice
Brad moving to the door. When she turned to offer
another apology and bid him good-bye, he was standing
only a few feet from her. A tiny gasp escaped as she drew
in her breath sharply.

Brad stepped down from the camper. "You will let him
come back later, won't you?" By his calculations, he had
only four more days to establish a positive learning base
for Timmy.

Her eyes felt glued to Brad's maleness and Jeni
couldn't seem to tear her gaze from his bare chest with its
dark, curly hair that she remembered was so soft, so
warm . . . She heard him chuckle softly.

"Yoo-hoo. O'Brien," he taunted, "wake up."

"I—I am awake," she protested awkwardly. "What did
you ask me?" The muscles rippled under his skin as he
moved to touch her arm. Veins stood out on his skin like
graceful paths for her emerald stare to follow. She almost
missed his question for the second time.

"I said, can Tim come back later?" Brad's hand paused
inches from her arm. Don't touch her, he lectured himself. For your own sake, don't touch her.

A slight trembling in his fingers drew Jeni's attention
to his hand. "You're cold," she said, noticing the morning
chill for the first time. "Go get dressed and do whatever
else you have to do, then let me know when you're ready
for Tim. I'll send him back."

Brad folded his arms across his chest. "Yeah. It is cold
out here," he agreed to cover the weakness in his character where this woman was concerned. "Tell Tim I'll be
ready in an hour or so, as soon as I fix myself some breakfast." He waited. There was Jeni's tailor-made opportu-

nity to invite him to breakfast. All she had to do was follow through.

She didn't. Pulling away, Jeni felt an actual grip on her even without Brad's physical contact. Each backward step was difficult. "Right. I—I'll go feed the holy terror so he'll be ready when you are."

"Right," Brad said blandly, watching her leave him. "You go do that."

Tim had barely finished eating when Brad shouldered a blue nylon pack and entered Jeni's camp. "Can Tim come out and play?" he teased lightly, a smile on his face.

The boy washed his hands at Jeni's insistence, dried them on his pants before she could stop him, and joined Brad.

"I've packed a lunch," Brad told Jeni. "If you don't mind, I'd planned to stay out most of the day."

Raising her shoulders she said, "No. I don't mind." It did bother her that Brad was saddled with Tim for the whole day, but she certainly couldn't phrase it that way. "Are—are you sure you want him the entire day?"

"I count only four more days up here for you two. Right?"

The thought crushed Jeni like a ten-ton weight. "Uh, yes. Why?"

"And you're going to Zion tomorrow?"

"That was my plan," she said hesitantly.

"Then I only have a couple more days to spend with my little pal here." Tim beamed up at Brad. "And I don't think taking a whole day is too much, do you?"

"No," she said tenderly, "of course not. If that's what you want to do." Brad was staring at her, and Jeni thought for a wildly ecstatic moment he might be going to add something about their former relationship.

"Good," was all he said. Taking Tim's hand, he led him down the road and out of camp.

Jeni sank desolately onto the picnic bench. Why should it suddenly unnerve her to be alone? she wondered. God, she felt awful with both of them gone. How quickly she'd adjusted to Tim's being a part of her life. He had rapidly gotten under Brad's skin, too, she marveled. At least, that was how it seemed to Jeni. Poor Brad, she thought. He decides to completely cut himself off from children and then Tim comes along.

Jeni also felt herself opening up to the possibility of truth in what Brad had told her about the learning problem he was so sure Tim had. It wouldn't hurt to check on it when she returned to California, she decided. Tim had displayed a deep-seated dislike of education that had to have its basis in something. All along, she'd imagined he was simply mimicking Alex. Maybe not, she thought now. Ignoring the problem, if there was one, would be doing a great disservice to Timmy.

She toyed absently with the coarse grain on the table top. It was time to plan, she mused, time to look ahead. All she'd worked toward in the past year had come to fruition; Tim was hers, she wasn't totally out of a job even though she'd had to make a concession there, and everything was falling neatly into place. Her blank stare fastened on the white, depressed ring mark on her left hand. Well, she admitted ruefully, *almost* everything.

With a sigh, Jeni stood, squared her shoulders, and started to clean up her camp. She glanced occasionally at the gold band on her right hand while the words Brad had spoken surged through her consciousness. Four more days, he'd reminded her. They had only four more days.

Jeni managed to amuse herself most of the day. A short trip to the visitors' center resulted in her decision to take Tim to the evening lecture, and when he returned at dusk he didn't object at all to her suggestion.

"So, what did you guys do?" Jeni asked as they made

their way up the road toward the visitors' center after dinner.

"Oh, nothin'." Tim skipped happily along beside her.

For a kid who'd supposedly hiked all day, he certainly had an excess of energy, she noted. "Nothing, huh?" she repeated. "Was it fun?"

Tim gave her a thoughtful look. "Sure."

Small patches of snow still lay in shaded spots where the sun seldom reached. Creamy white columbine shared the shelter of the clustered pines while mountain bluebells grew lushly around the perimeter of the clumped trees. Tim spotted a low-growing yellow flower that had opened for the night instead of closing like the others.

"What's that?" he asked, pointing.

Racking her brain, Jeni finally dredged up a name. "That's called an evening primrose, I think," she said. "I looked at a lot of pictures of wild flowers, today, but I'm pretty sure I remember that one correctly."

"Oh." Tim paused thoughtfully. "Does primrose start with a P?" he asked.

Jeni was startled at the question. "Why, yes, it does."

"Good," he mumbled.

The visitors' center was built near the edge of a precipice, its wide viewing windows overlooking the Wasatch formation that gave Cedar Breaks its name. Tim seemed to be looking at the canyon, so Jeni took him over to the rail fence bordering the sheer drop. In the distance, a deep red and purple sun was setting over Cedar City.

"Isn't it lovely, Tim?" she said, awe-struck by the beauty of the craggy depths. Gnarled junipers clung tenaciously to the cliffs, a mute testimony to the erroneous naming of the canyon by early settlers who mistook the junipers for cedars.

He gripped her hand tighter. "I guess so." Looking up

at her, he expressed a childish fear. "Don't fall in," he warned.

Jeni smiled down at him. "Don't worry, honey. I'll be careful. I promise."

Tugging at her hand, Tim urged her away from the cliff edge. "Let's go."

"Sure, Tim," Jeni said, complying with his wishes.

It was warm in the small room used for the lectures, and Jeni took Tim's jacket from him before removing her own. There were only two seats remaining. Following Tim's lead, Jeni made her way to the empty chairs in the second row.

"Oh, boy!" Tim exclaimed, plopping himself happily down next to the man in the third chair. "Hi, Brad."

Brad's answer was for Tim, but his eyes caught and held Jeni's. "Hi, pal."

Jeni seated herself next to Tim, on the aisle. She started to ask him if he'd known Brad was going to be there, then decided against it. After all, coming to the lecture had been *her* idea in the first place. Any thought of collusion on Tim's part was nonsense.

A large movie screen was unrolled in the front of the room and Tim squirmed from side to side before turning to Jeni. "I can't see," he complained.

"Shhh," she told him. "You'll be able to see enough when the show starts." Jeni looked at the broad-shouldered man in the chair in front of Tim. Chances were the boy still wouldn't be able to see. "Try sitting on your knees," she suggested.

The folding chair squeaked noisily, nearly dumping Tim in a heap. Both Jeni and Brad reached for his arm, lifting him free of the tangled mess of the partially folded chair.

"I'd give him my seat," Brad said, "but . . ." He gestured at the person in front of him, who was nearly as large as the man blocking Tim's view.

Jeni realized she was acting silly. A child occupied the chair in front of her. Tim could easily see if he sat where she was. "Come on, honey," she told Timmy, "sit on my lap."

"Aw, that's sissy," he objected vociferously.

"Yeah, sissy," Brad taunted softly. "Give the poor kid your seat, lady. I won't bite if you sit over here by me."

She made a disgusted face at Brad just as the lights dimmed. "Okay, okay. Switch seats with me, Timmy."

The exchange was made quickly. In the darkness, Jeni felt Brad's presence envelop her. She closed her eyes involuntarily.

"You'll never see the slides that way," he whispered in her ear, his warm breath fanning wisps of her hair across her cheek.

Jeni jumped at his nearness. Turning her face to him, she discovered how close their lips were, scarcely hearing as a ranger began to explain each slide in a hypnotic drone.

"You're as jumpy as a frog on a hot griddle," Brad observed. "Here." He began to rub the back of her neck with one hand, his arm casually draped across the back of her chair. "Better?"

"Mmm. Yes." He'd chosen an interesting analogy, she thought, recalling a similar one she'd once heard: If you drop a frog into hot water, he'll immediately jump out and save himself, but if you put him in a pot of comfortably cool water and warm it slowly, he won't realize he's in trouble till it's too late.

Which incidence described her relationship with Brad Carey? she wondered. More important, which one did she *want* it to be? Jeni was suddenly very tired—tired of fighting her feelings, tired of lying to herself, tired of fleeing. The water was warming on the poor frog slowly, she mused, and she found she didn't care.

Slowly, gracefully, she let her head fall to rest on

Brad's shoulder. His hand closed over her arm, pulling her closer. It was such a little thing, this surrendering to him, yet she felt the weight of the world lifting from her mind, her body, her spirit.

Tim reached over, finding her hand. As Jeni held his smaller hand, sheltered in Brad's arms, she sighed contentedly. It was going to be all right. By the time the water got hot enough to be fatal, her vacation would be over. Why not enjoy it until then? She straightened in her chair as the lights came on.

"Let's go there," Tim said.

Dreamily, Jeni asked, "Where?" to Tim's obvious consternation.

Brad chuckled softly. "I think you missed the show, O'Brien," he teased. "Tim wants to go see the alpine pond. Right?"

"Uh-huh," Tim said, appearing glad that someone had been paying attention.

"Okay," Jeni easily agreed. "When?"

"Now?" The boy considered more carefully. "No, we can't. It's too dark. How about tomorrow?"

"I think you and Jeni are going to Zion, tomorrow, Tim," Brad reminded him.

"Not necessarily," Jeni quickly offered. "We could go to the pond instead."

"Could we?" Tim asked excitedly. "Brad too?"

Jeni slowly turned to Brad. "If he wants to come with us, I think I'd like that very much," she said.

"You're sure?" Brad's voice was low and serious.

"I'm positive." Her eyes had become a deep emerald green. "Please come with us."

He nodded affirmatively, helping her to her feet, his hand at her elbow. "Tell me, O'Brien," he whispered in her ear. "What were you thinking about while everyone else was watching the show?"

"Frogs," she said whimsically, "and hot water."

*   *   *

"Why didn't one of you guys tell me this trip would take hours?" Jeni complained, struggling up a slippery trail that was partially covered with snow.

"You should have paid attention last night," Brad said. "The ranger warned you."

"It's four miles," Tim volunteered brightly. "Neat, huh?"

"Four miles?" she groaned. "Oh, no."

Reaching back for her, Brad offered his hand, grabbed hers, and hoisted her up a steep incline. "Come on, O'Brien. You can't let a little kid show you up, can you?"

The icy snow and mud made the going slow until they'd reached a leveling-off point. Jeni was out of breath, but proud she had kept up, especially after all Brad's teasing.

"Whew!" she gasped, leaning on his shoulder theatrically. "Some hike. Where's the pond?"

"Hey, Tim," Brad called, "how much farther?"

The boy turned to look at a worn brown sign, his lips moving, his brow furrowed.

"Brad, he can't——"

Brad shushed her. "Wait."

"It says, 'Alpine P-pond, one mile,' " Tim told him. "Come on. Last one there's a rotten egg!"

Jeni stared, open-mouthed, after Tim, then wheeled to face Brad. "You said he couldn't read. You lied to me!"

"Whoa," Brad said. "He couldn't."

"Don't tell me you taught him in the space of a few days. Nobody's *that* good." Placing her hands on her hips, she waited angrily. "Well?"

"He's got a long way to go, Jeni. That's why I didn't want you to push him. He still has the differing vowel sounds to learn, plus blends, silent letters, and a lot more, but he's on his way, because *now* he believes in himself."

"You're serious," she observed, scowling.

"Dead serious." Brad fell into step beside her. "Let's catch up with Tim and I'll tell you what's happened." Filling her in on his efforts with her son, Brad seemed thoroughly satisfied with the boy's progress.

"He really couldn't read, then, could he?" she asked, walking hand in hand with Brad. "I suppose that's why he always seemed disinterested in the books I bought him."

"Of course. He'd learned one thing well in school: how to fake his way through and cover his shortcomings. He made big noises about not caring, but he really did care. Now, he can be honest with you, like he is with me. If he doesn't know an answer, he'll ask. Be sure you answer him seriously no matter what he asks, so he doesn't feel stupid for asking."

"I will." She stopped, still gripping Brad's hand. "I—thank you," she said sincerely. Placing her hands on Brad's shoulders, Jeni kissed him lightly.

Brad was staring at her, his eyes glowing a deep, inviting chocolate. "It was my pleasure," he said soberly. "He's quite a kid."

"I thought you didn't like children," she said in a near whisper.

Shrugging his shoulders, Brad turned away. "He's okay—for a kid. I was just glad I could help." Damn. Why had he put it that way? Brad wondered absently. Because, he realized, he couldn't very well tell Jeni he loved that boy like he was his own. Things were complicated enough between them without adding a stupid confession like that.

Jeni chose to ignore Brad's latest slur about children. The real point was that he *had* helped Tim. In a way, doing so when he felt as he did was a bigger sacrifice, a nicer gesture.

"I want you to write down the names of those tests Tim

needs so I don't forget them," she said, breaking the silence.

"I will," he promised. "How much longer do we have?"

She knew he didn't mean time on the trail. "I'll be starting for home the day after tomorrow."

"I see. Well, maybe I'd better do it tomorrow." He stopped walking. "Jeni, I——"

Placing her fingertips on his lips, she shushed him, then stood on tiptoe and kissed him tenderly.

As his arms crept around her, she deepened the kiss, letting herself melt against him, forgetting for the moment that they weren't alone.

The slushy snowball caught Brad in the back of the head, splattering Jeni's cheek.

"Gotcha!" Tim hollered.

Brad recovered first. Shaking the slush out of his hair, he bent to scoop up a handful of snow. "I guess if you combine a city kid and snow in the middle of summer, you're bound to have some problems," he said, molding the dingy snow into a ball. "Here." He handed his effort to Jeni, then made himself another. "I think we owe our young friend something, don't you?"

"You bet," she hissed, clenching her teeth. "And when I catch him is he going to be sorry."

"Leave a little for me," Brad said, laughing. "I owe him too, remember." He caught up with her. "He interrupted the nicest kiss I've had in, oh, let's see, at least two or three hours."

"Oh, he did, did he?" she mocked, drawing back her arm to throw. "In that case, here."

Brad ducked and Jeni's snowball sailed down the hill to splat against a tree. "O-o-oh," he drawled, "you want to play rough, do you?"

"Now, Brad," she wheedled, backing up the slope, her hands outstretched in a plea for mercy.

"Hey, Mom," Tim called, "you got a problem?"

"Yes, Timmy. Help!" Jeni shouted. She felt a soft snowball hit her in the back. "Timmy! Whose side are you on?" Spinning around to face the boy, she turned her back to Brad and was immediately plastered with his snowball.

"All right," she said under her breath. "No more nice. That's all, fellas." She ducked behind a tree. Let them close in for the kill, she thought, I'll be ready when they do.

Signaling to Tim to circle around, Brad went the other way. Jeni got Brad first by decoying his attention long enough to pitch one onto his chest. Enough snow slid down his collar to keep him busy for a while.

Now for Tim, she told herself, her arms loaded with quickly assembled snowballs. When she spotted him, she threw in such rapid succession he barely had time to return fire once.

Timmy sputtered, dancing around and shaking snow from his hair, face, and clothing.

"I see you don't need my help," Brad said, coming up behind her. "You've repaid the little stinker by yourself."

"Yup," Jeni said proudly. "I got him."

"She doesn't play fair," Tim complained.

Brad laughed heartily, slipping his arms around Jeni's shoulders. "Considering what we were doing when you started this, I'm surprised that's *all* she did to you."

"Oh yeah? What were you doing?"

"Shall we show him?" Brad asked.

Jeni lifted her face to his, leaning against him, and offered her softly parted mouth. "You think we should?" she whispered. "He's only eight years old. I wouldn't want to corrupt him."

"Better now than when he's older," Brad answered

He joined his lips tenderly to hers, but the kiss was rather short-lived.

They both broke into gales of laughter when Timmy loudly exclaimed, "Yuck!"

Brad fought to control his smile. "You're not supposed to giggle when a man is busy making love to you, O'Brien," he said. "It's too hard on the guy's ego."

"Sorry." Laughing, Jeni looked from Brad to Timmy and back. "I really did mean what I said," she told Brad.

"About corrupting him?" he asked wisely. "I know." Putting his arms lovingly around her, he whispered, "I promise not to do anything he hasn't already seen on TV. Okay?"

Jeni elbowed him in the ribs. "No!" she countered, thinking of all the bedroom scenes she'd seen lately on television. The thought of herself and Brad together, like that, made her knees weak and her head spin.

"Come on, *Mom*," Brad said, giving her an affectionate squeeze. "The kid is getting ahead of us."

"Right." Sighing, Jeni took Brad's hand and started after Tim.

Brad hadn't sounded too upset or jealous when he'd mentioned Tim just now, had he? At least he understood her feelings about propriety where her son was concerned. The little guy had seen enough unusual relationships in his young life. There would be no excuse for her adding to his confusion. A stable family structure was what he needed, and Jeni intended to provide it. Being a parent required sacrifices all along the way, didn't it? she asked herself. Of course it did. She'd known that from the start, determining to do whatever was necessary to be more than an adequate parent. She'd expected to gladly do without some luxuries for Tim's sake, realizing that a child would monopolize her time. And she'd seen that having Tim around would change her priorities. That went without saying.

Jeni gazed wistfully at Brad's back as he led her up the trail. What she hadn't known was how hard it would be to give up the first love she'd felt in years. More than that, it would have to be accomplished unemotionally so that Timmy never suspected what she'd done, and why. A tear escaped down her cheek and she quickly wiped it away. Saying good-bye to Brad without showing her feelings was probably going to be the most difficult thing she'd ever tried to do.

She squeezed his hand, conscious of the warmth and gentle security of his touch. There had to be a way to make the break painlessly, her mind insisted, but her body denied it.

Chapter Eleven

Jeni's legs ached that night, but not nearly as much as her heart. The day *had* been marvelous, she decided, glad she'd asked Brad to go along. It wouldn't have mattered, she saw clearly, whether he'd have been with them or not; she'd still have felt every bit as attracted to him—as in love with him—as she felt now. Past the point of anger with herself for losing her heart to Brad, she was nearly numb from the overwhelming torrent of emotions bombarding her. Sitting close to the fire for warmth, she rubbed her sore muscles.

"Did we work you too hard?" Brad asked pleasantly.

Jeni nodded slowly, staring at the leaping orange and yellow flames.

"Looks like you're not the only one," Brad said. He pointed to the dozing Timmy. "Your son is pooped out, too."

"So I see," she answered softly. "Brad, I . . ."

He closed her in a tender embrace, cradling her against himself. "I know, honey, I know," he whispered. "Don't think. Just sit here with me and enjoy the fire."

You're not going to cry, Jeni told herself sternly. You are *not*. She leaned back, fitting herself into Brad's arms. "It was good, today, huh?" she asked in a quiet voice.

"Mmm," he murmured in her ear, "very good." His

arms covered hers, his fingers absently toying with her ring. "I think Tim had fun, too, don't you?"

Jeni nodded. "It's going to be difficult for him when we leave here," she said. "I don't quite know how to handle it." She felt Brad's arms tighten around her.

Of course, she was concerned about Tim, he thought. That was only natural. Still, it hurt that Jeni hadn't mentioned that she'd miss him, too.

"How can I help?" Brad asked. "You know I'll do whatever I can to make it easier for him."

Easier for Tim, she mused cynically. Sure. Let's all make it easy for Tim. What about her? an inner voice screamed. Who was going to make it easier for her?

After long moments of silence she made a suggestion. "You could leave first." She might be able to control herself if Brad were the one who drove away.

Brad seemed to hold his breath for a second, then he sighed. "Okay. When would you like me to go?"

Damn you! Jeni's defenses cursed. You don't have to agree. You could argue, or fight, or something! She got control of herself before she spoke. "We'll be here until the day after tomorrow. There's no hurry."

"I suppose not," he replied. "I've got my gear pretty well organized. It doesn't take me long to pack up." Rocking her slowly in his arms, he stared into the fire. Picturing their parting was almost too much to bear, and he struggled to redirect his thinking before his emotions got the upper hand.

Jeni was no less affected by their conversation and closeness. She purposely broke the spell. "I should put Tim to bed. He's liable to catch a cold lying out like that."

Releasing her, Brad rose. "I'll do it. He'll be too heavy for you."

Beyond arguing, Jeni watched Brad hoist Tim in his arms and tuck him into bed. The boy barely stirred.

Stiffly, she stood up. "I probably should turn in, too."

"Probably," he echoed. He'd returned to the fire, but made no effort to touch her again. "Tim's really sound asleep," he told her, knowing she'd sense his double meaning.

"You know I can't," Jeni said. She glanced over at the camper where she'd come alive again after so many years of only half-existence. "He might wake and miss me."

"I suppose so," Brad said with very little conviction. "You know, Jeni, you'll have to start living your own life again sometime."

Sadly, she faced Brad. "Tim has only been with me for a few days, and we both heard him awaken and call for me. What if I hadn't been there?" Jeni bit her lower lip to control its quiver.

"As much as I hate to admit it, I guess you're right," Brad conceded. "Will I see you tomorrow, or are you still planning to go to Zion?"

"I—I don't know," she answered truthfully.

"Well, whatever," he said. "Good night."

She took several quick steps after him, her arm reaching out, then stopped. No. She mustn't succumb to personal weakness. She'd spent a lifetime forming the convictions that made her what she was. They couldn't simply be set aside for a whim, no matter how deep her emotional involvement. Was that all Brad was to her? she wondered, just a product of her overactive emotions? As much as Jeni wished she could accept that definition of him, she knew he was more. Much more.

The blond ranger stopped at Jeni's camp when she spotted Tim. "Good morning," she said. "I didn't realize you had a boy."

"He wasn't here at first," Jeni explained, setting Tim's breakfast in front of him.

"We're having a special nature study walk for youngsters this morning—" she checked her watch—"in less than an hour. I thought he might like to join us."

"Well, I don't know," Jeni said. "We were going to take a drive to Zion."

"Oh. Well, if he decides to go, we're meeting at the visitors' center at nine. We'll be returning about noon."

Thanking her, Jeni sat down by Tim. "Do you want to go?"

"Uh-huh. Sounds fun." He stuffed a bite of pancake in his mouth.

"I'd have to feel sure you'd behave yourself," she warned. "No funny stuff."

"I swear." Tim raised his hand.

"We'd have to leave early tomorrow in order to see Zion on the way home. You wouldn't mind?"

He shook his head. "Nope."

Patting him on the back, she said, "Okay. Eat all your breakfast so you don't run out of energy. Then I'll walk you up to the visitors' center."

"How long do I have? Time for more pancakes?" Tim asked.

Jeni chuckled. "I think you can manage to eat a few more." She poured batter onto the hot griddle. "Bring me your plate."

It was with a certain trepidation that Jeni watched Tim march away with the other children. Two rangers kept the group well in hand, she noticed, relaxing a bit. She'd decided not to apprise them of Tim's background, afraid it might prejudice them against him when his behavior differed very little from the other children's. He deserved a clean slate, and she was going to see he got it.

Rounding the corner into camp, Jeni looked toward Brad's campsite. If his truck hadn't still been there she would have suspected he'd left, since she'd seen no sign of life all morning. Perhaps he'd gone for a walk, alone.

Or maybe he was still asleep—still in bed. Jeni's heart leaped to her throat, pounding uncontrollably at the image.

Her feet carried her to her own camp, habit making her clean up the breakfast mess. She stared repeatedly at his camper. Maybe he wasn't in there. Sure, she decided, he's not there.

But what if he is? she fantasized. Suppose I go and knock on the door and he opens it, and . . .

She looked at her watch. "Just after ten," she mumbled, reaching for her hairbrush. "Almost two hours."

A lot of things could happen in two hours. Jeni's hand rested at her throat and she felt her pulse begin an erratic race through her veins. The idea wouldn't be stifled. Brad was so close and she felt so empty. Damn it—she needed him. What kind of fool would pass up an opportunity that had so miraculously appeared?

Straightening, she stepped slowly over the rocks between the campsites. Jeni's hand poised, ready to knock on his door, then she lowered it. This was silly, it was absurd, it was—it was what she honestly wanted to do, she admitted nervously. Quickly smoothing her hair, she tucked her sweater neatly into the waist of her jeans, took her courage in hand, and knocked on the door.

No one answered. Suddenly, Jeni felt stupid, very awkward, and just a little sullied. It had been wrong to come to Brad in the first place. Well, he'd never know she'd been there. She'd simply go back to her camp and forget all about this. She'd . . .

Brad opened the door, revealing his half-dressed, disheveled appearance.

"I—I thought you weren't here," Jeni stuttered.

"I had a little trouble deciding to answer your knock," he said. "I didn't get much sleep last night, and . . ."

Jeni wheeled to flee. "Forgive me, Brad. Really, I didn't mean to bother you."

He caught her arm. Lifting her up beside him, he grasped her tightly. "Do you have any idea what you're doing to me?" he demanded. "Why do you suppose I didn't sleep?"

Wide-eyed, she stared at the turbulent emotions racing across his expressive face.

"Because of you, Jeni. That's why," he continued. "I spent the whole damn night wanting you, needing you, and then you come knocking on my door like an answer to my prayers. What am I supposed to do? If I let you in, I have to keep away from you, and I don't know if I can do that. Do you understand? That's why I didn't open the door at first." Perspiration was beginning to stand out on his forehead.

Raising her hand, she gently caressed his cheek. "Oh, Brad," she whispered, "hold me."

"What about Tim?" he asked, peering over her shoulder, expecting to see the boy standing outside.

"He's on a hike," she murmured against his bare chest.

"Alone? How could you——"

"The rangers have Timmy," she quickly told him. "It's an organized group hike." Lowering her voice, she added, "He'll be back around noon."

Brad tilted up her face, looking deeply into her eyes. "And you came to me?" he asked haltingly.

Jeni nodded.

"To stay?" he rasped.

"If that's what you want," Jeni whispered.

"Is it what *you* want?" he asked, breathlessly kissing her neck and shoulder.

"I'm here," she reminded him. "That should tell you something."

"Ah," Brad murmured, "it tells me dreams come true. There really is a Santa Claus."

"In July?" she teased as she closed the door behind her.

Brad was smiling wistfully. "Uh-huh. You *are* my present, aren't you? I remember asking for a doll just like you."

She giggled, playing with the hairs on his chest. "Boys aren't supposed to play with dolls, silly."

"Little boys don't. In case you haven't noticed, I'm a *big* boy."

Jeni slipped her hand between them, caressing his evident desire. "So, I see," she began to taunt.

Groaning, Brad pressed her to him in desperately escalating need. "Oh, honey, I love—" He stopped himself when he felt her start to resist, to pull away. "I love it when you do that," he said, completing the sentence in a way he felt she could accept.

She did. For a moment, Jeni had thought he was going to say he loved her, and she waited expectantly to hear the words that never came. But it was better this way, she rationalized. In the beginning, she'd assumed Brad would be a "fling." Why should she be upset if that was exactly the way it turned out?

"Kiss me," she said. "You talk too much."

Lifting her sweater over her head, he cast it aside. "I still can't believe you're here, like this, now. I thought we'd never get another——"

"Shut up, Superman," Jeni nagged lovingly. She pulled off her bra, tossing it on top of the discarded sweater, and pressed her warm, full breasts to his chest.

"Ahh," he groaned, his hands grasping her around the waist, then sliding up to cup the sides of her breasts. His thumbs slid between them to tease her nipples and Jeni writhed against him, losing herself in the ecstatic feelings he was awakening in her.

The speed of her arousal amazed her. She must have needed him much more than she'd imagined, Jeni thought vaguely. Much more. With her hands on his lower back, she pulled him hard against her, tilting herself to meet him at the same instant.

Brad tore at the rest of her clothing, then his own. He was acting like a man possessed, and Jeni reveled in every moment of it. Wrapping his arms around her, he drew her down on top of him on the bed, his mouth joining hers in a twisting, consuming kiss.

She met him with the same urgency, the same desperation he was showing her, as if holding tight would somehow postpone their inevitable parting. As he carried her once again to the heights of pleasure they'd found together, Jeni's final cry was a mingling of her climactic ecstasy and a wail of despair for her ultimate loss; a protest against the lie of "happily ever after."

And they held each other close as their last minutes ticked away.

"Brad," Jeni said tenderly. "Brad?"

His dark head had fallen onto her arm as he slept with one leg pinning her to the mattress.

It was nearly noon.

"Brad, please," she urged, feeling the coarse hairs on his leg as she slid out from under him. Poor thing, she thought, he's exhausted from his sleepless night. Well, maybe it's better this way.

Dressing quickly, she twisted the door knob, hoping it wouldn't wake him. As the door came open, she was seized with an uncontrollable urge to stay. Tiptoeing back to Brad, she drew a blanket over him, savoring the sight of the clean, masculine lines of his body for the last time. Her lips brushed his and she felt tears gathering in her eyes.

Fleeing out the door, she closed it silently. Well, that was that, she agonized. Time was up for her and Brad. Tim would be with her the rest of the day, and tomorrow morning . . .

The moisture in her eyes cascaded freely over her cheeks. Cursing her loss of control, Jeni wiped her eyes and started slowly for the visitors' center to claim Timmy. Every time she felt she had her emotions firmly in hand, another batch of tears would pool in her lashes, then slip out to further condemn her failure and escalate her mounting fury.

Unreasonably angry with her own weakness, Jeni was still a quarter mile from the visitors' center when she saw the hapless Tim coming toward her. How *dare* he disobey and leave the rangers? she fumed.

Stalking menacingly up to the boy, she shook him. "What do you think you're doing? You promised me, and now look what you've done. You could get hurt alone on the road like this." By this time she was nearly shouting, not realizing her anger was misdirected.

Totally confused, Tim made no reply.

"Do you hear me?" she shrieked.

Timmy nodded rapidly.

"Well, what do you have to say for yourself? And it'd better be good," Jeni threatened. "Well?" She gave him another shake.

Tears had started to fill Tim's eyes. "The ranger said to," he muttered.

"What? Don't you lie to me, Tim," she warned. "Don't you dare."

"I—I'm not," he stammered. "She said since you were late you probably wanted me to walk home. She said to be careful, and I was."

"Late?" Jeni blasted. "I started out in plenty of time, so let's have the truth. Now."

"But——"

"No buts," Jeni warned him. "It's not even . . ." She looked quickly at her watch, expecting to find it was well before the scheduled time to call for Tim. It was nearly twelve-thirty. Jeni's mouth fell open. It must have taken her ages to tear herself away from Brad and walk from camp. When she saw Tim's tears, his distraught expression, she fell to her knees, hugging him fiercely.

"Oh, Timmy, I'm sorry," she sobbed against his shoulder. "I was mistaken."

Hesitantly, he stroked her back, his small hands doing their best to fix whatever it was that seemed to be so terribly wrong.

Facing him, Jeni wiped her eyes, then his. "You know I love you, don't you, Tim?" she asked, her voice breaking.

His arms crept around her neck for the first time. "I—I love you, too," he confessed with a sob. "I love you, too, *Mom*."

Chapter Twelve

It wasn't the chill in the afternoon air that woke Brad, it was the lack of Jeni's unmistakable nearness. She'd gone, just like that, he realized angrily. The least she could have done was to have the decency to say good-bye. . . . He peered out the camper window at her camp. No one seemed to be there. Well, she'd asked him to be the first to leave, he remembered wryly, and now was as good a time as any. Dressing hastily, Brad began to stow his gear.

Mindful of her puffy, reddened eyes, Jeni purposely skirted Brad's camp, but Tim's curiosity drew him to the man's side. "Hi."

Barely glancing back, Brad continued to pack. "Hi," he said gruffly.

"You goin' fishin'?" the boy asked.

"No."

"You goin' home?"

"No."

"You mad?" Tim questioned sensibly.

"No!"

"Oh," the boy said. "I got some good news. Wanna hear it?"

I'm glad *somebody* does, Brad mused cynically. Well, it isn't the boy's fault his mother stomped all over my feelings by walking out on me, is it? He sat down and gave Tim his attention. "Okay, pal. Tell me."

"She loves me!" Tim exclaimed. "She said so."

Brad had to turn away, clearing his throat noisily, to control his all too evident involvement. He was going to lose the two most important people in his life, and he'd only now fully acknowledged it.

"Isn't that great?" Tim asked.

"Yeah, pal," Brad managed to choke out. "That's great."

"I said I loved her, too," Tim proudly announced, "and she cried."

Nearly undone, Brad went back to packing his gear.

"I figured out why she cried before," Tim said. "I'll bet it was love then, too."

Brad froze. Out of the mouths of babes, he thought to himself. "What makes you think so, son?"

"Oh, I just do." He looked seriously at the big man. "I love you, too," he said happily.

That did it. Brad drew him into a tight hug. Fighting to set a manly example, he blinked back the moisture gathering in his eyes. "Guess what, pal," he said, forcing a smile, "I love you, too."

"And you'll write to me?" Tim asked.

"Sure thing." Remembering the testing information he'd promised Jeni, Brad took paper and pencil, quickly jotting down the things she'd need to know while Tim looked over his shoulder. "Give this to your mom, will you? And be sure to have her write your address for me so I can send you your picture and a letter once in a while."

"Okay!" Tim skipped exuberantly home with the piece of paper. Watching him go, Brad had to turn away.

Tim slapped the paper on the table. "Brad sent this," he announced, "and he wants my address to write to me."

"Oh." Jeni said dully, lost in her own misery. "Terrific."

"Yeah," Tim told her. "He loves me."

"Now, Tim," Jeni warned carefully, "just because Brad's been nice to you doesn't mean he loves you."

"But he does. He said so."

Jeni couldn't believe her ears. "He what?" Oh, how despicable. What an awful deception to pull on a child. It would make his leaving so much more traumatic for Timmy. Brad had no right to say that, no right at all, she fumed. What could he possibly have hoped to gain by it? Except perhaps . . . No. He wouldn't try to use Timmy to get back at her, would he?

"Write down my address and I'll take it to him," Tim persisted.

Gathering her turbulent emotions behind a facade of calm, Jeni said, "No, honey. *I'll* take it to him."

Jeni hit the table hard with the paper and the flat of her hand. It made a resounding whack.

"What was that all about?" Brad asked curtly.

Jeni purposely lowered her voice. "What's the idea toying with Tim's emotions? He trusted you!"

"So?" Brad's teeth clenched, his jaw muscles working.

"So? Why lie to him?"

"I didn't."

"Oh no?" Jeni hissed. "Then why did you say you cared about him?"

Brad closed his fists. "I didn't say that, I——"

"Well, he thinks you did," she interrupted. "What exactly *did* you say?" Glaring at him, her expression dared him to talk his way out of this one.

Speaking softly, Brad looked her straight in the eye. "I said I loved him." His gaze never faltered.

"You *hate* kids, Brad Carey, so don't go trying to convince me you love that one!" She gestured wildly toward her son.

"Why not?" he shot back. "*You* love him."

"I'm his mother," Jeni said firmly.

"And before? When he was only a lost kid on the streets with nobody who gave a damn? What then, O'Brien?"

"So what?" she said, her tone rising. "That's not the point here, is it?"

"Then what *is* the point? Tim and I hit it off, that's all. He's a great kid with a heart as big as a house, and I'd like to keep in touch, come to see him once in a while, watch him grow into a great adult. What's your real objection, Jeni? Are you afraid to let him care for anyone but you?"

"No!" She couldn't go through the years with Tim, always wondering if Brad might drop in, or listening to Tim extol Brad's virtues like he had the last few days. There was simply no way she could take that much pressure, loving Brad the way she did.

"I want you to leave him alone, that's all. Do you hear?" she exploded defensively. "Drop it. He's young. He'll forget about you quickly enough."

Hurrying past Timmy, she shut herself in the tent, intending to wait there till she'd heard Brad drive away.

Fury and despair built inside Jeni as her helpless feelings grew. While she'd been expressing her anger to Brad, her mind had been focused on protecting Timmy. Now, in the enforced quiet of the lonely tent, her own yearnings surfaced and she cursed the nameless dread and emptiness threatening to swallow her up, heart and soul.

Closing her eyes, she threw back her head, clenching her fists. How had she let herself love Brad? From the beginning she'd known it couldn't last. Why hadn't she stopped herself? Why—why?

With a deep, ragged sigh, she sank down against the

rumpled sleeping bags. Because, she thought, loving Brad had seemed so right, so perfect, that the impossibilities of their relationship had taken a backseat to her innermost desires, the part of her that had wanted and needed him so badly.

Jeni bit her lip. She still did need him. And how long would she love him? she wondered. Instantly, a one-word answer came to her: *Always*.

Brad was sitting on the picnic bench, his elbows on his knees, his hands clasped in front of him when Tim joined him, striking the same pose.

"Hi."

Sighing, Brad returned the greeting. "Hi."

"Is she mad at you?" Tim asked.

"Looks like it," Brad said.

"Why?"

"It's kind of complicated, son," Brad told him. "Don't worry about it, okay?"

"Okay." The boy grew pensive. "Why do you call me that?" he asked.

"Call you what?"

"Son. I wish I was."

Tousling Tim's hair, Brad said, "So do I."

"Hey!" Tim shouted. "I could be, huh?" He got to his knees on the bench, facing Brad at eye level. "All you'd have to do is marry her." He pointed at the tent.

Brad shook his head, laughing softly, sarcastically. "It's not quite that simple, Tim. People don't usually get married because some cute kid wants them to."

"Oh." He thought for a moment. "Doesn't she have sex appeal?"

"What?" Brad nearly jumped off the bench.

"You know," Tim explained seriously, "like that toothpaste commercial says you have to have." He sang the familiar jingle.

Struggling to keep a solemn expression, Brad said, "Oh, I see." He was positive Jeni wouldn't want him to continue this particular discussion with the boy, but if he didn't, Tim was likely to talk to her about it, and that would be much worse.

"First," Brad began, "the man and woman have to be in love."

Tim leaned on his elbows. "Oh. You don't love her, huh?"

Oh, boy, Brad thought, this is getting sticky. "Well, that's not exactly right, Timmy," he said truthfully. "I think the problem is, she doesn't love me."

"Oh. What else?"

"Well." Brad cleared his throat. "Then there's the business of whether their lives will fit together. Like, if one has pets and the other hates animals."

"We don't have any pets," Tim volunteered. "Do you?"

"Maybe that was a bad example," Brad told him. "Look, it's like this with your mom and me. She needs a home and a steady life in one place, and I don't even have a house."

That seemed to shock the boy. "You don't?"

"No. I sold everything and I live in that camper."

"You don't work?" Tim asked.

"Not now," Brad explained carefully. "But I'm going to. When I find a place I want to stay, I intend to buy a pizza parlor and run that."

"Wow!"

Brad smiled. "You like pizza?"

"Yeah. And you could give Alex a job. He used to work in a pizza place till he got busted the first time. Then nobody'd hire him. But *you* would, huh, Brad?"

"Well, sure, pal, if you'd vouch for him." A plan was beginning to form in Brad's mind. Why not? he thought.

At least he'd be trying to help other kids like Tim who might not get a fair chance anywhere else.

Tim had jumped up and was heading for Jeni's tent.

Shaking his head, Brad put the last few things in the camper, looked over his deserted camp, started to climb into the cab of his truck, then paused. Tim hadn't really said good-bye. When the boy came back out, he'd wave, then leave, Brad decided. Resting against his camper, he crossed his arms to wait.

"And we don't have pets, so it's okay," Tim babbled.

"What *are* you trying to say, Timmy?" Jeni demanded, her patience almost nonexistent.

"Brad's going to buy a pizza parlor and we can all live there—even Alex—cause we don't have pets, and he says it's okay if you don't have sex appeal cause he loves you, and you don't have to love him, and——"

"Whoa!" she yelled. "*What?*"

Her shouting subdued Tim somewhat. "Sorry. I forgot, Brad said you were mad at him."

"Well, that part you got right, anyway," Jeni grumbled, crawling out of the tent. "Stay there," she told Timmy as he started to follow.

Straightening in the warm afternoon sun, she tried to force herself to relax and be objective about Brad. How much had Tim understood correctly? she wondered, and how much was childish wishing?

Speaking of wishing, she thought cynically as she spotted Brad leaning nonchalantly against his truck. Bravely, she sought to capture his gaze. If only half of Tim's babbling had had some basis in fact, she knew she'd be a fool not to pursue it.

Overwhelming love replaced her dwindling anger as his eyes met hers, the magic as compelling as ever. If she was ever going to find out how he really felt, this was the time.

"Hey, Carey," she shouted across the camps, "what do you mean I don't have sex appeal?" She could see the color rise in his cheeks. "Well?"

Brad shuffled his feet. Obviously, Tim had enlightened her about their recent man-to-man talk.

Jeni wasn't through. "And what do you mean telling the poor little kid I don't love you, when I *do*?!"

That brought Brad to attention. "You do?" he called back. "Who says? You, or the stinker?"

"Me!" she exclaimed as she ran toward him.

Brad's arms opened invitingly and he swung her around, off the ground.

"Did he have the part right about you loving me?" she asked breathlessly.

Brad nodded. "But I never said you weren't sexy," he added.

"Then where . . ."

"From a toothpaste commercial," Brad told her. "And I *do* love you, Jeni O'Brien. More than I'd ever thought possible."

"We're going to live in a pizza parlor with Alex?" she asked with a smile.

Brad laughed deeply and with genuine relief. "Not exactly. I think the only part he got right was when I told him I loved you."

"Thank goodness," she sighed. "That was the best part. Why didn't you tell me before?"

He kept his arm around her possessively. "I figured you had Tim, and your life was well-ordered without me. I don't even have a place to call home. Besides," he added, "I wasn't smart enough to see how much I loved you till I felt it was too late to do anything about it."

"No, 'love at first sight'?"

"I fought it," he admitted, "but I lost."

"Me too," Jeni confessed. "I didn't think it was possible you'd want the two of us, especially after all you said about kids."

"Wow," he sighed. "We almost blew it."

"Yeah, we almost did."

They both noticed Timmy's broad grin from across the campsite as he peered out of the tent. "You don't suppose he knew what he was doing, do you?" Jeni asked.

"No," Brad said. "I think he just wanted a family."

She slipped her arms around Brad's waist. "To my mind, we fit that picture." Kissing him, she whispered in his ear.

"Please, madam!" he replied, feigning shock, "not till we're married."

"That brings me to my next question," Jeni said with a smile. "Are we going to get married before we live in the pizza parlor, or are we going to wait?"

"Do you suppose, if I have another father-to-son talk with Tim, he'll understand our sharing the camper for one night while we plan the wedding?" Brad asked.

"Plan the wedding, or the honeymoon?" she teased.

"Look, lady, if that kid knows about sex appeal, there's no telling *what* else he knows. I doubt our disappearance together would surprise him much."

Jeni looked over at Tim. "You know," she said slowly, "you're probably right."

"Don't burn your marshmallow, Timmy," Jeni warned. The fire seemed warmer than ever before with all three of them there. She leaned back against Brad.

Tim made a face. "I think I burned it."

"Watch me," Brad instructed. "I'm an expert."

"Sure," Jeni said with a laugh.

"Who was talking about marshmallows?" Brad whispered wickedly.

"I was," Tim said loudly.

Brad flushed slightly. "Oops. He has excellent hearing, I see."

"What about that little talk you were going to have with him?" she asked. "Have you yet?"

"No. To tell you the truth," Brad confessed, "I don't quite know how to put it to him without having it sound, well, you know."

"I know," she said wryly. "I've been thinking about it, too. I suppose we *could* wait till we get home."

"You, maybe. I'd be a raving maniac."

"Speaking of home," Jeni continued, "what are your plans? Are you going to follow me to my place and park in the drive?"

"I don't know," Brad gibed. "Does your house have a side door that doesn't squeak?"

"It squeaks," Tim piped up.

Giggling, Jeni covered her mouth.

"Thanks, son," Brad told him.

"Welcome. When are you guys going to get married?"

"Are you in a hurry?" Brad asked the boy.

"Sure. I want you to come live with us."

"Me, too," Jeni said softly, snuggling closer to Brad.

He put his arms around her. "It won't bother you if I buy you a new house, will it? I kind of wanted to do that for you."

"No pizza place?" Tim wailed. "I thought——"

"Not to *live*, pal," Brad said. "The pizza parlor will be a job, a place to work where I can give Alex and kids like him a chance to make a fresh start."

"You were serious, then?" Jeni asked. It had seemed like such a perfect solution, she could hardly believe it had really happened.

"Sure. Actually, it was Tim's idea, but it was a darned good one. As a professional, honey, do you think it'll work?"

She kissed him soundly on the mouth. "Yes, Brad. It's

a beautiful gesture." Expecting Timmy to comment on her show of affection, Jeni looked over at him. His eyes were barely open, his head drooping lower and lower. She nudged Brad gently. "Look."

Tim's head jerked upright, then sagged once again. He stifled a yawn.

"You ready for bed?" Brad asked.

Jeni suppressed the urge to answer for herself as Tim nodded.

Scooping the tired little boy up in his arms, Brad carefully placed him in his sleeping bag, then closed the tent flap. Timmy didn't stir.

"He's sound asleep," Brad said. "He seems a lot more relaxed tonight."

"I'm not surprised, are you?" she said. "He now has a father to look after him as well as a mother. He's doubled his security." Jeni paused and stared longingly at Brad. "I'll bet he sleeps clear through till morning without waking."

"You think so?" Brad asked, lifting her to stand in his arms.

"I think so," she said seductively.

"And you?" Brad whispered.

"I bet I'll hardly sleep at all," she said. Taking his hand, she started toward the camper and the life she'd almost thrown away. A sudden anxiety seized her, then passed. It was going to be all right, she told herself. Brad squeezed her hand in affirmation of her decision, her love.

"I do love you," he said quietly, "both of you."

Jeni closed the door, coming to him in the darkened camper. "I know, Superman," she said. "I know."

RAPTURE ROMANCE

*Provocative and sensual,
passionate and tender—
the magic and mystery of love
in all its many guises*

COMING NEXT MONTH

SHADES OF MOONLIGHT by Laurel Chandler. Spirited Tria O'Connor had always relied on her second sight for guidance—but nothing could prepare her for England and Sir James Carfax. Though his manner was typical of a gothic lord, his embraces were anything but Victorian. But this practiced lover was rumored to have all the women he wanted; did Tria stand a ghost of a chance at winning his love. . . ?

OCEAN FIRES by Diana Morgan. When Dan Quincey reeled beautiful oceanographer Veronica Coyne out of the sea and into his net, they soon became caught up in a magical affair. And though Veronica swore she wouldn't be tied down, she couldn't deny she was hopelessly in love. . . .

A CHERISHED ACCOUNT by Jeanette Darwin. Tax returns, yes— love affairs, no. Specializing in straightening out artists' financial tangles, accountant Megan Saunders swore never to mix business with pleasure— until she met sensual, challenging Garth Matthews. Yet even as he colored her life with brilliant strokes of passion, Megan knew in her heart and in her head that partnership with an artist was a risky venture. . . .

HERE THERE BE DRAGONS by Marianne Clark. Globe-trotting TV newsman Gabe Whitfield was everything a woman could want—and everything Rachel Novak feared. But in a night of love, her body betrayed her in the arms of this man who lived only for the moment and promised nothing more. Still, Rachel wasn't sure if she could trust him—until he left and she discovered how achingly empty she felt. . . .

RAPTURE ROMANCE

Provocative and sensual,
passionate and tender—
the magic and mystery of love
in all its many guises

New Titles Available Now

(0451)

#81 ☐ **TENDER BETRAYAL by JoAnn Robb.** From their first electrifying embrace, ballerina Monica Bradshaw knew she'd been fated to spend life with Holt Gallagher. But Holt had been badly hurt by another dancer long ago, and Monica wondered if his past heartache would destroy the love they now shared. . . . (129946—$1.95)*

#82 ☐ **AN UNLIKELY TRIO by Kasey Adams.** Taking a short vacation before becoming a mother to her newly-adopted son, Jeni O'Brien wasn't looking for men. But when she met Brad Carey, Jeni was shaken with a burning passion. Yet even as she reveled in Brad's embrace, Jeni was afraid. Was there enough love in their romantic duo for a third. . . ?
(129954—$1.95)*

#83 ☐ **THE LIGHTENING TOUCH by Megan Ashe.** Kristin Cole vowed she'd never get involved with another mountain climber, until the lightening touch of expert mountaineer Dan Norris filled her heart with desire. Their affair was sensual fireworks— until her skill on the mountain surpassed his and he pulled away. Would Kristin have to choose between being the best . . . or being loved. . . ? (129962—$1.95)*

#84 ☐ **A PRIORITY AFFAIR by Andra Erskine.** When Fallin O'Hara met handsome financier Preston Smithwick, her instincts cried danger. Fallin had had her fill of high pressure career men, but she couldn't fight Preston's appeal. As they tumbled into a heady affair, Fallin feared she was caught in the love-web of a man who'd pull her back into a world she no longer wanted. . . . (129970—$1.95)*

*Price is $2.25 in Canada
To order, use coupon on the last page.

RAPTURE ROMANCE

**Provocative and sensual,
passionate and tender—
the magic and mystery of love
in all its many guises**

RAPTURE ROMANCE

*Provocative and sensual,
passionate and tender—
the magic and mystery of love
in all its many guises*

**Buy them at your local
bookstore or use coupon
on next page for ordering.**

RAPTURE ROMANCE

Provocative and sensual, passionate and tender— the magic and mystery of love in all its many guises

---

RAPTURE ROMANCE

*Provocative and sensual,
passionate and tender—
the magic and mystery of love
in all its many guises*

**Buy them at your local
bookstore or use coupon
on next page for ordering.**